CHRYSTAL FALLS 5

A LOSS OF INNOCENCE

Meredith Hill

SCHOLASTIC INC.
New York Toronto London Auckland Sydney

ISBN 0-590-33744-0

12 11 10 9 8 7 6 5 4 3 2 1   1   6 7 8 9/8 0 1/9

Printed in the U.S.A.   06

CHRYSTAL FALLS 5

A LOSS OF INNOCENCE

The Wrong Side of Love
Breaking the Rules
The Bad and the Beautiful
The Morning After
A Loss of Innocence
Forbidden Love
A Night to Forget

Chapter One

Dawn Newhouse sat back on her heels and looked at the boxes piled around her. Then she shrugged, grinning in such a foolish way that she was glad no one was there to see her. She had dreaded this moving day for weeks, only to have it turn out to be fun.

Pete Carter had come to see her and the new house. He hadn't stayed long, of course, but he *had* driven by to see her. Naturally he had been pressed into service by her brother Josh, who had been unloading the rented truck out in front. If she closed her eyes she could still see Pete smiling at her from the doorway with Josh's stereo under one arm and two speakers piled up under the other.

"Special delivery," he had announced, laughing at her startled expression. "Where do I put these?"

"Oh, anywhere," she told him. Then, reconsidering, "Up in Josh's tower. I'll lead you."

Since her mother and brother were nowhere in sight, she swung to her feet, stood on tiptoe, and planted a quick, warm kiss on Pete's mouth.

"Foul," he cried. "Catching a guy with both arms full."

She laughed and led him along the hall and up the circular stairway. She ran ahead quickly, wanting to see his face when he saw this wonderful room set high in the tops of trees, with windows on all sides.

"Wowee!" he said, staring around in amazement. "You didn't fight your brother for this? You're crazy. It's great, something else." Recovering, he set down his load and turned to her.

"Hey, Newhouse," he said, holding out his arms.

She didn't need any second invitation. Pressed against him with his face against her hair, she closed her eyes with ecstasy. How could she love this wonderful, strange guy so much? But she did, and she had from her first glimpse of him those brief months before when she had moved to Chrystal Falls with her mother and brother.

When she thought about it, which she did most of the time, she realized that nothing had ever really come between herself and Pete except the town's bitter social currents. As much as she despised the snobbery and hatred of this place, without it she would never have

2

met Pete Carter and known how joyous she felt in his arms.

How many times had she and Pete come together like this, only to break up miserably? She had learned not to look at tomorrows, just to take the wonderful todays, like this.

"Hey," he said softly, lifting her chin with his finger and looking tenderly into her face. "Much happiness here, okay?"

"Much happiness," she whispered, hugging him tighter for a delicious moment.

Then Josh had called from below and Pete had gone on his way, leaving even moving day wonderful by his having been there. The move from their apartment into the house at 13 Timberline Drive had been going on, in pieces, all week. On Thursday the furniture stored back at their old home was delivered. Friday after school Dawn, along with her brother Josh and her cousin Tim, had managed to get the beds set up and the furniture in place. Now, in midafternoon on Saturday, they were beginning to see the light. Josh had been bringing another load of the final things in the rented truck when Pete came.

Dawn hastily pulled a box nearer to begin work again, as her mother passed the door with a huge arm load of clothes. "Hi, Doc," Dawn called to her mother. "How are you doing?"

Barbara Newhouse stopped, braced her burden against the doorway, and blew a strand of her dark hair out of her eyes. "All right for a beginner," she said.

"I feel like an old hand at this," Dawn

laughed. "Look at me. I lived in the same house for sixteen years and here I am moving for the second time in a matter of months."

"Don't worry about getting to be an expert," her mother said. "There is no way I ever intend to go through this again."

As her mother went on down the hall, Dawn stared after her. She hadn't thought about the new house as a place her mother would stay forever. As for herself, who knew? She shrugged and began folding sweaters into her bottom drawer.

You have to feel at home somewhere to stay there forever. Would she ever really feel at home in Chrystal Falls? One thing for sure, she didn't hate it the way she had when she moved here.

She shuddered even remembering that first move. She and Josh had been prepared to help their newly widowed mother set up a new medical practice in this Pennsylvania mill city where their uncle already lived and practiced. They had not been prepared for the swift, brutal social currents that divided the town as dangerously as the Rapid River divided the city. In Chrystal Falls there were Mill people and Hill people, with no mixing if Dawn's Aunt Vicki and Pete Carter were to be believed.

Pete Carter. None of that, girl, Dawn cautioned herself. Just thinking about Pete set her daydreaming again. Pete, with that dark, intense expression, the way his mouth tightened when he smiled, and unfortunately, his stubborn belief that nothing of value, not even their love, could survive the pressures that divided Chrystal Falls so viciously. Never mind that, she assured herself, someday she would win him around for good!

The drawer was almost filled when the honk of a car horn brought her to life.

"Help, help," a voice cried from the door. "Dawn. Josh."

Chelsea Chrystal.

Dawn swung to her feet, smiling. No one in the world could make such simple words sound so exciting. Chelsea was the undisputed princess of the city. The Chrystal house was the handsomest estate on the Hill that the Mill people hated so deeply. Her ancestors had founded the town, and her family still owned and ran the ugly mills, belching smoke on the north side of town. As if it wasn't enough to be rich, socially powerful, and the most beautiful girl Dawn had ever seen, Chelsea was also just plain fun.

"Party, party," Chelsea was calling, banging at the door. Chelsea was wearing what every young cover girl wore on moving day, immaculate white creased jeans, a scarlet sweat shirt, and a red-and-white bandanna tied pirate-style around her glossy blond hair. And one gold loop earring.

"I bet you thought I lost the other earring," Chelsea crowed. "For heaven's sakes, open this door. My arms are dropping off." She preened at Dawn. "Don't I look like a genuine pirate with only one earring? I tried it in my nose, but it hurt."

Dawn's mother, drawn by their voices, reached around Dawn to let Chelsea in. "No wonder your arms hurt. What in the world are you carrying?"

"A party." Chelsea laughed. "How are you, Dr. Newhouse? I hope you are ready for coffee because I brought you some."

Dawn took the thermos from Chelsea and nodded toward the kitchen.

"How wonderful!" Dawn's mother said, as Chelsea covered the kitchen table with potato chips, a coffee container, and an immense covered tray. "What in the world?"

Chelsea started to uncover the massive plastic tray, then paused.

"Before I do this, could I please use your phone?"

Barbara Newhouse groaned. "I wish you could. They somehow failed to get it hooked up. I am living with only a beeper until Monday."

Only the briefest shadow of concern crossed Chelsea's face before she shrugged and pulled the cover off the tray with a dramatic flourish. The platter was heaped with quarter sandwiches studded here and there with little burr gherkins, ripe and stuffed olives, and carved radish roses.

"Isn't it beautiful?" Chelsea asked. "I got every kind of sandwich I could think of . . . cucumber, roast beef, tuna fish, and egg salad with curry. The rye ones are ham with Dijon. Then there are turkey and braunschweiger on pumpernickel — "

Before Chelsea could finish this recital, an imperious rap at the front door startled her into silence. As Barbara Newhouse started for the door, the knocking began again, even more angrily than before.

Dawn stared in disbelief. Alexander Chrystal, Chelsea's father and usually the calmest, most gentlemanly person in the world, stood in the doorway, his face white with fury. His voice, usually so elegantly controlled, trembled with anger.

"Forgive this intrusion, Dr. Newhouse, but is my daughter here?"

Chelsea was instantly at Dr. Newhouse's side. "Dad," she cried. "What's the matter? What's wrong?"

"You know very well what's wrong, Chelsea," he said. "You were told to let us know where you were! You left without any message we could find. I have been searching for you since a little after two. We only now found your car out there."

"I just got here," she explained. "I forgot about leaving word. Then I went to the deli." She waved toward the kitchen. "I wanted to surprise Josh and his family with an afternoon snack. Dad, you wouldn't believe how slow they were at the deli. I thought they'd never get this ready."

"I don't want to hear excuses," he told her. Turning to Barbara Newhouse, he bowed slightly. "Please forgive this intrusion and my unfortunate tone. I was deeply concerned. I am afraid I must insist that Chelsea come home immediately." Glaring at Chelsea, he said, "You will follow my car."

"But, Dad," she protested. "I haven't even seen Josh!" The color had risen furiously in her face, staining her cheeks the shade of her sweat shirt. "I don't understand. I just got here."

"You will follow my car," he repeated, turning away with a swift, curt motion.

Chelsea seemed torn between anger and tears. Dawn caught her arm and hugged it. "We'll see you later. Thank you so much."

The color left Chelsea's face as swiftly as it had come. Her full mouth tightened and she stood very severe. For that brief moment, she looked like her own angry father. "I don't have to take this kind of treatment," she said hotly. She glanced at Dawn's startled face and looked away. "I'm so sorry," but as she spoke, her eyes flashed. "But I don't have to take this, you know. I really don't."

In spite of her rebellious words, Chelsea made a quick apology to Dawn's mother and left. She backed the car out of the drive with a screech of rubber just as Tim and Josh came up Timberline Drive with a new truckload of boxes from the apartment. Tim braked, and both of them stared after the retreating convertible, frowning.

"What's with Chelsea?" Josh asked, coming up the steps two at a time. "She didn't even

8

wave. She didn't even act as if she saw us." His effort to keep the hurt out of his voice wasn't very successful. Although Chelsea and Josh had been drawn to each other from the first, only very recently had they dated on a regular basis. As whimsical as Chelsea was, Dawn didn't blame Josh for a certain nervousness about his status as number-one boyfriend.

"I doubt if she did see you," his mother said quietly. Dawn silently agreed. If Chelsea had not been blinded by fury as she spun out of the drive, she probably had been by tears.

"But what happened?" Josh pressed.

"A mystery," Dawn said, not understanding what she had seen well enough to explain it.

"In words of one syllable," Josh pressed.

This wasn't fair. To explain how strangely Alexander Chrystal had acted would take longer words than that and a lot more of them than Dawn was ready to come up with.

When she tried to explain, the words came out awkwardly. "Mr. Chrystal pulled a heavy father act because he didn't know where Chelsea was, and she hadn't checked in or something." Then Dawn remembered Chelsea's request to use the phone when she first came in. "Apparently she was delayed a long time at the deli when she went to pick up a picnic for us."

Tim frowned. "That's not like Mr. Chrystal," he said. "He's usually not into public scenes." Dawn studied her cousin thoughtfully. Since Tim had grown up in Chrystal Falls and known Chelsea's family all his life, his amazement only deepened the mystery.

"Didn't used to be," Josh said thoughtfully. "Maybe all this trouble Mr. Chrystal had with Monty has worn his patience thin."

Dawn silently opened cold drinks and passed the sandwiches. Josh could be right. Chelsea's older brother Monty had torn the town apart with a wild criminal spree. His arson and lying had ended in his being carted away somewhere to keep him out of prison. She flushed at the memory of how his incredible charm had blinded her into letting him use her in his dreadful schemes. She had been lucky to get away with only humiliation.

"And I never heard about Chelsea's having to check in anywhere before," Tim went on. "I wonder what's up."

Dawn shivered. "Something that Chelsea doesn't mean to take lying down," she predicted. "Come on. Everyone dig into this gorgeous food. It's the least we can do after the trouble it has caused for Chelsea."

Chapter Two

Chelsea, fighting back tears, spun her convertible onto Timberline Drive, pressing the accelerator as hard as she dared. Since the Chrystal family home was on the hill across the river, she was used to steep, winding roads. But Timberline was different. Instead of being lined by handsome mansions set back behind formal drives, this road wound between dense woods, dark and forbidding. It was narrow, too, with no bridle paths along the side for horseback riding.

The squeal of her tires was satisfying. She wanted to squeal or scream herself. How could her father have treated her like that in front of her friends? Why would he want to treat her like that at all?

A few days before, she and her younger sister Amy had listened patiently to his ponderous announcement that he wanted to know where they were at all times. "Just tell someone responsible," he had said. "Your mother or grandmother or a member of the staff. If you are going to be delayed, call home so we will know."

No matter how silly his rule was, she had meant to obey it, if only to humor him. She really had meant to call. Was it her fault the Newhouse telephone hadn't been installed yet? Possibly she could have called from the deli, but who would have thought he would wheel out his car and come chasing after her as if she were a runaway dog? Thank goodness Josh hadn't been there to see that scene. She tightened her shoulders at the thought. She would have died of shame if Josh had been there.

From the sounds of traffic she realized she was nearing a main road. She slowed a little as she went into the next curve. She almost didn't see the man in time. He stepped from the trees almost directly into the path of her car. As she slammed on her brakes, the car shuddered and rocked from side to side, swerving to the right as she locked her wheels.

She trembled with shock, and her heart pounded furiously as the man stood right against the car, staring down at her. The bill of his cap threw his face into shadow. What she could see of his face filled her with an overwhelming sense of menace — heavy, tangled brows; a rough, untrimmed black beard; and eyes brilliant with hatred. He gripped the side of her car as she tightened her hands on the steering wheel to brace herself.

"You fool," she cried, her voice rising to a tone of hysteria. "You fool! What do you mean by walking out in front of my car like that? What in the world is the matter with you?" Then, threatened by his continuing silence, an awful second thought struck her. "Are you all right? Are you hurt?"

"I *could* have been killed," he said. His voice was gravelly and deep and not at all friendly.

"But you —" she began.

He ignored her. "I could have been killed but maybe you could have been, too." He paused, his eyes never leaving hers. "Nobody's safe."

She stared at him. He wasn't making any sense. Everything about him was terrifying. Yet he was holding on to the side of her car so firmly that she couldn't just drive away without dragging him along after her.

"Let go," she said, as threateningly as she could. "Let go of my car right now. What do you want?"

"People get killed all the time," he went on, as if she hadn't spoken. "Cars explode when they are started. A big house like the one you live in would go up like a torch if someone fired it."

She stared at him, not believing her ears. His words were wild and unreal but he seemed sane. She knew the sound of irrationality in a man's voice. She would never be able to forget those horrifying weeks that she had been called every night by an unbalanced man.

13

This was different. This man was in control. Somehow his calmness made his words even more horrible.

"What do you want?" she asked again. "Please, please let me go. Don't hurt me."

His lips moved in something like a smile. "I got no call to hurt you. It's your dad who owes me, and it's your dad who's gonna pay. Or else."

"Pay?" she asked. This was robbery, then. What did she have? Maybe ten dollars after that trip to the deli. And her watch. She turned her left arm on the steering wheel to expose the slender, gold, engraved watch her grandmother had given her for Christmas. Why hadn't she worn her gold chains? They were worth a lot. Her father had even had them insured.

"I have some money," she stammered. "And this!" She slipped off the watch and offered it to him.

He took it, turning it in square hands studded with heavy black hair. "Pretty," he said. "But not enough." She shivered. "I aim to get what your dad owes me, or else."

He glanced at the sky, darkening with rain clouds. "Clothes. I need warm clothes, too, and the money he owes me. Five thousand dollars."

The amount staggered her. But if she could just hold him off, maybe a car would come. Hadn't she seen a truck pass just after she left Dawn's house?

He laughed, a short, mean laugh. "You figuring on paying your daddy's debt? Somebody better had, I tell you. Him or somebody. All I'm asking is what he owes me. Enough to make a new start, that's all." He looked again at the threatening sky. "The first is clothes. Maybe you could get me some warm stuff right away. Then work on the money."

"I'll try," she promised. "Just don't harm my family. Please don't hurt any of them. I'll get the clothes right away, tonight. But how will I reach you?"

His laugh was short and ugly. "And let you bring me uniforms with the cops still in them?" He paused, as if he were thinking. "Tell you what. You get the warm stuff and stow it in your car. Then when I get in touch, you'll be ready."

As he stepped back, he slid his hand into his pocket. No, Chelsea's mind registered. Don't let him have a gun.

He drew his hand out again with a lighter concealed in it. She only realized what he was holding when a jet of blue-and-yellow flame shot into the air. The flame was close enough to blind her for a moment and fill her head with the stench of butane gas. She cried out and pulled back.

"Just don't be stupid, Chelsea Chrystal," he said ominously. "Those big houses go like torches. And all that's in them goes up in smoke."

The light went out as swiftly as it had risen. As suddenly as he had come, he stepped back from her car, those cold eyes still on her face.

"Please!" she cried after him.

"Just get the stuff," he said.

Her hands were wet on the steering wheel as she pulled away. She was sobbing without tears, and her legs felt weak and rubbery. In the rearview mirror she saw him watching her, a dark, threatening mass in the shadow of the trees.

She saw her father's silhouette in the open door as she pulled into the drive. She had never driven so carefully as she had the rest of the way home. Think. She had to think what to do. By the time she was crossing the bridge that separated the town from the mansions on the hill, she had made her decision. She would tell her father what had happened. By working with the police, the man could be trapped and put away like the mad telephone caller had been.

As she stepped from the car, her father walked across the porch toward her. "I was beginning to worry again," he told her. She could tell how much effort it took for him to keep his voice calm. "Come in, your mother and I want to talk to you."

"Dad," she began, gripping his arm.

He shook his head. "I know I was rude and I'm sorry. Worried parents sometimes behave badly."

His lips were smiling but his eyes were dark with concern. "Come on, we have been waiting for you. I'll have Ben take your car around to the garage."

It was not a full family council, since her

16

grandparents were not there. Her mother was obviously dressed for the evening, wearing the famous Chrystal pearls in a cascade down the front of a mauve taffeta dress. Amy was cross-legged on the floor with a game of Solitaire half played in front of her.

"I have a speech to make," her father said, as Chelsea slid into the chair by Amy. "I'd like you to hear me out. Then, if you have questions, your mother and I will try to answer them."

He didn't sit down but stood by the piano. It was as if he were in court, presenting a case. His words were carefully selected, his tone reasonable and convincing.

"Here in the family we can openly admit that our position is one of prominence. While there are great advantages to such a position, it also has its drawbacks. People of wealth and power make enemies. It was out of concern for your safety that your mother and I decided to set the new rules . . . that we must know where you are all the time, that you must call in any change of plans. The decision was good. Our mistake was in not explaining why we were doing it."

Then he paused. "We insist that you keep these rules."

"You have an enemy?" Amy asked.

He smiled and looked at his wife. "More than one, I fear."

"But if you know who he is, can't you just have him arrested or something?" Amy asked.

He shook his head. "He has done nothing

but make threats. Loose talk is not a criminal offense. In fact, most loose talk leads to nothing except the caller making himself feel important."

Chelsea caught her breath. Now was the time to tell him what had happened on Timberline Drive. Before she could say anything, Amy spoke again. "Can't you talk to this man, maybe pay him to go off about his business and let us alone?"

His glance was sharp with disapproval. "Amy," he said. "I am astonished at you. The Chrystal family settled this valley, bringing civilization and law into these mountains. We have stood for those things ever since. Your grandfather is a judge, I am a lawyer. Payment like that is extortion. No Chrystal would ever pay a single cent for such a lawless purpose."

Twilight had fallen. Her mother snapped on the desk lamp, flooding the room with light. Chelsea saw her father's face clearly, rigid and indignant at Amy's suggestion. He's wrong, she told herself miserably. He hadn't seen that man's face, the glitter of hatred behind that swift flame of fire.

"Now," he said briskly, relaxing and touching his palms together. "We agree that you will be careful to keep our rules until we tell you otherwise. Your mother and I are going out, but the cook is still here. Amy, if you would please call your grandparents to dinner?"

The moment had passed. Chelsea watched

her father lean to offer his wife his arm as Amy shot upstairs to do his bidding.

"Question, Chelsea?" he asked, turning to her from the doorway.

She saw the same stubborn intensity in his face that the man on the road had had. "No," she told him. "No questions." The difference between the two men was that the bearded man had nothing to lose and her father had everything.

At that moment she knew what she had to do.

Chelsea heard the faint hum of the tv set from downstairs, as she went through Monty's closet looking for warm clothing. She tried to remember how big the man had looked. To be safe, she chose only ski sweaters, which were designed to fit over other clothing. She wrapped gloves and a scarf and two knitted caps inside the bulky down jacket and let herself out of Monty's room. After listening a moment, she went on tiptoe down the back stairs to store the clothing in her car.

Chapter
Three

Dawn rarely slept well the first night in a new place. By the time the last box from the move was emptied, she was sure she could have crawled into the empty carton and not stirred until morning. Aching in places she didn't know she had muscles, she went straight from a steaming bath into her bed. She heard an owl call in the woods beyond her window, and the dog, Abner, bark once or twice.

Then her mother was calling her softly but insistently as she shook her shoulder. The color in the woods beyond the window suggested morning, but the room was still dark enough that her mother's face was in shadow.

"Apparently I am needed in Emergency. My little beeper went off and I have to fly," her mother whispered. "Josh is taking me over to the hospital. Do you want to ride along?"

"At this hour?" Dawn cried, hugging her comforter closer.

Her mother laughed. "I wasn't sure you would want to be here alone without a phone, while this place is so strange to all of us."

Dawn peered at her sleepily. "You're right," she decided. "I really don't. I'll be right there." By the time she got to the kitchen, Josh was out warming up the car.

"I hope this emergency isn't anything bad," Dawn told her mother.

Barbara Newhouse shrugged. "You know just as much about it as I do. Without a phone to call in on, all I know is that I'm needed."

Timberline Drive was dark and deserted. An opossum lumbered across the road in front of the car, its eyes green circles staring back at the headlights. Josh let his mother out at the door to Emergency, then turned to Dawn.

"The hospital cafeteria is open all night. Want coffee or something?"

"Gosh, yes," Dawn told him. "I didn't even think of money."

He grinned and rattled his pockets. "I'll even buy. Maybe we can find out what's up with Mom and when we can expect her back."

The coffee tasted so good that Dawn had another. She meant to pay Josh back for it, but the woman behind the counter shrugged the money away. "Save it," she said. "You brought Doc Barb in, didn't you? I heard they sent for her to handle the emergency that came in off the Hill."

Dawn had the coffee back at the table before the words registered.

"The Hill," Dawn repeated, going back to the counter. "Where on the Hill? Who called?"

The woman wiped the counter as she replied. "I don't know where," she said. "But I understand Alexander Chrystal called and especially asked for your mom."

Back at the table, she cautioned Josh, "Now listen, don't jump to a lot of crazy conclusions, but let me tell you what that woman just told me."

He clearly ignored her warning. His eyes widened a little and he caught his lip between his teeth. "It can't be Chelsea," he said. "They would have said so if it was Chelsea."

"Hey, hey," she said, touching his hand. "We've been here a half hour. We ought to be able to check this out. How about the phone?"

He frowned at her a moment and then laughed, realizing what she was suggesting. One of the mysteries of the hospital was that you could get information easier by phone than in person. All the nurses would ever tell you was that someone was "doing as well as could be expected." Over the phone you sometimes got a fuller report.

As Josh dialed the hospital switchboard from the phone in the lobby, Dawn squeezed in beside him. Even that close she could hear his request but not the answers he was getting. After asking for Dr. Barbara Newhouse and getting some answer Dawn couldn't hear, he tried again. "Is Dr. Walter Gilbert available?"

Dawn could make no sense of Josh's side of

the conversation as he talked to their Uncle Walt, but Josh's voice lost that high edge of concern. That must mean that Chelsea wasn't involved. Then it struck her that Josh was really being pretty cool about all this. What if she had reason to believe that something had hurt Pete Carter terribly? She leaned against the side of the phone booth, a little ill at the thought. When Josh replaced the receiver, he turned to her with relief.

"It's not Chelsea," he said. "Thank heaven for that. But it's really strange. I mean, strange."

"Come on," she said. "Don't give me adjectives. What's going on?"

He took her arm and steered her toward the door. "I'll tell you about it going home."

Dawn reminded him as he turned from the parking lot into the street. "Tell me what you heard."

Josh smiled, amused by her impatience. "Mom couldn't come to the phone because she was talking to the cops."

"*Cops!*" Dawn echoed.

He nodded. "Uncle Walt said some hunter out after rabbits tripped on the alarm wire that runs around the Chrystal place."

"*Alarm wire!*" she said, amazed.

He frowned over at her and went on. "This would be easier to tell without an echo," he told her. "Anyway, when the guard challenged him to halt, the hunter panicked, ran with his gun, and shot himself in the leg."

"Guard!" Dawn said, in spite of herself.

"Boy, you *are* having problems," he said, grinning at her. "I bet you need protein, maybe bacon and eggs. The guard was some guy I never heard of, a Zacchary somebody."

"But Zacchary's not a guard," Dawn protested. "He's the new stableman that Mr. Chrystal hired to help out Ben with the horses. They are going to get Amy a jumper and Mr. Chrystal explained that Ben already had more work than he could handle."

"If he wasn't a guard, why was he carrying a gun and going around shouting, 'Halt'?" Josh asked as he turned onto their road.

When Dawn just looked at him, he shrugged. "Just another mystery, like Mr. Chrystal blowing his stack yesterday over not getting a phone call from Chelsea. So now we have two mysteries."

Dawn unlocked the unfamiliar front door and stood back to let him in. "Three mysteries," she corrected him. "There's never been an alarm wire around that place before. Amy and Chelsea and I go back and forth over the borders of the place all the time. I would have seen it."

"Three mysteries," Josh conceded. "Let's make a fire in our new fireplace and have breakfast. Surely three mysteries are worth two eggs over with bacon?"

"I'm only doing this because you always cook my eggs too hard," she told him.

The warm wooden walls and deep windows of the new house had looked cozy and inviting by day. In this bleak light the rooms seemed

24

to grow into immense caverns. The windows not yet touched by sun were black and forbidding. She used the scraps of wood Josh had gathered by the hearth to start a fire. By the time the logs he brought in began to crackle with flame, the bacon was crisp and the toast ready to be buttered. They used a hassock for a table by the fire and sat on the floor.

"Don't you even have a theory as to what is going on up at Chelsea's?" she asked.

"Whatever it is will be singing along the grapevine by noon."

Dawn groaned. "I forgot! Did we really promise to have lunch with Uncle Walt and Aunt Vicki today?"

The thought of spending even an hour or two at their uncle's house made Dawn cringe. She had expected to dislike her cousin Tim from the things his mother had said about him. Instead, it was Aunt Vicki herself whom Dawn couldn't bear. Her uncle's wife was a bargain table of unpleasant traits. Snobbish, vain, conceited, her Aunt Vicki had it all together on the negative side of the ledger.

The siren awakened Chelsea first. The thin, high wailing rose and fell as it came nearer along the hill road. Before she could get to the window, Amy had burst into her room, her dark eyes wide with terror.

"What is it, Chelsea?" she asked. "Is it that man, the one Dad was talking about?"

Chelsea, halfway across the room, caught Amy in her arms and stood stunned at the thought. She almost dragged Amy with her to the window.

The ambulance had made it into the circular drive in front of the house. Her father, tall and trim in his navy bathrobe with the monogrammed pocket, was talking intently with two men in uniform. A patrol car sat off to the side; its lights circling steadily made the tops of the trees bloom with color.

At least Chelsea could see that her father was okay. She tightened her arms around Amy with relief. "Is it that man, the one Dad was talking about?" Amy had asked. A burst of wild hope leaped inside her. Maybe it was the bearded man. Maybe something awful had happened to him. Maybe he had even been killed, and she wouldn't have to find all that money and hide what she was doing from her family.

"Look, Chelsea," Amy whispered. "The light in the woods."

Chelsea watched the beam of the flashlight move toward the drive through the trees. Only when it was near enough to fade into the outdoor security lights did Chelsea see the men who were following the light. Two men carried the stretcher while a third one ran alongside, holding something in the air, a bottle of something that was fastened to the man being carried.

She wanted to see the injured man's face. She wanted the man on the stretcher to be the bearded man from Timberline Drive. She held her breath as the little caravan approached the ambulance and they lifted the stretcher in.

Amy had begun to cry softly against her side. She patted Amy. Amy of the tender heart, Amy who loved horses and dogs and her family and her friends with a vast blanket of warmth like sun on a summer day. What would Amy think if she knew that Chelsea was only disappointed that the unconscious man on the stretcher was the wrong man?

He is making a monster of me, she realized in horror. But nobody will protect my family from him but me. Nobody.

As the ambulance started back down the hill, Chelsea saw her father drive out behind it with Zacchary, the new stable hand, in the seat beside him. She and Amy had started for the door to go downstairs when their mother rapped softly at the half-open door.

"There you are," she said to Amy, who flew into her arms.

"What is it? What happened?" Amy asked.

Chelsea could see her mother straining to find the right words. "A hunter," she finally said. "Apparently he had come for rabbits. He tripped on a wire. When Zacchary answered the alarm, the young man refused to stop and ran away. Somehow this hunter managed to shoot himself with his own gun."

Chelsea registered the strange words silently, watching her mother's face. Amy heard them, too. "Wire?" she asked. "What alarm? What was Zacchary doing up?"

Elizabeth Chrystal took a long, deep breath. "Must we talk about this now? It's not even dawn yet."

"Yes," Amy said in a desperate tone.

Chelsea's mother sighed. "Very well, dear. Your father had a temporary alarm system installed around the premises. The bell rings out in the stable by Zacchary's quarters. Now, can't we all just go to bed?"

"Will he die, that young hunter?" Amy asked.

Her mother stroked her hair. "Probably not. He's only unconscious from loss of blood."

After Amy let her mother lead her away, Chelsea lay in the dark of her room and watched dawn come through the tops of the trees. How afraid her father must be of this man, to install an alarm system secretly like that, to have the new stable hand stationed to hear it even at night. The bearded man who had stopped her there on Timberline Drive was just as dangerous as she had feared. And nobody would do anything about sending him away but her.

She had never cried quite like that before, without sobbing, without having trouble with her breath, just huge, helpless tears leaking out of her wide-open eyes, making a widening dark stain on her rose-colored pillowcase.

Chapter Four

Dinner at her Uncle Walt and Aunt Vicki Gilbert's house was as infuriating as Dawn feared it would be. Aunt Vicki, dressed in a ridiculously youthful pantsuit with a stock scarf that she kept having to adjust, shrugged off the safety fence and the guard as being perfectly natural precautions for the Chrystals to take.

"Surely you realize that Bill Gurney was released from state prison just last week. He swore publicly to get Alexander Chrystal when he got out of prison. Why shouldn't Alexander have the right to protect himself and his family?"

"What did Gurney go to prison for?" Tim asked. "I guess I never heard that story or have forgotten it."

"It was a long time ago," his father told him. "You were just a kid when he was convicted of embezzling a fortune from the

29

Chrystal Mills. He got a ten-year sentence and railed at the press about coming back and getting Mr. Chrystal for pressing the suit."

"He was guilty, wasn't he?" Tim asked. "What did he expect?"

"A slap on the hand," Aunt Vicki broke in. "Those people think the world owes them a living."

Dawn concentrated on her plate to keep from having to meet her aunt's eyes. She wondered how many people from the other side of town her Aunt Vicki had ever known. The Mill people Dawn knew didn't think the world owed them anything but a decent chance. She remembered too clearly how awful it had been for her friend Karen Pickett when her father had been laid off at the mill. Karen and her brother had both worked at the country club and been humiliated shamefully just for trying to help out at home.

Finally her aunt tired of that subject, only to go on to an equally unpleasant attack on the new house on Timberline Drive. Dawn just tuned her out for fear she wouldn't be able to hold her tongue. But she watched her mother's noble attempt to look interested in her sister-in-law's raving.

Barbara Newhouse looked exhausted. She had stayed with the wounded young hunter at the hospital until almost noon. She had barely had time to shower and dress before it had been time to come with Dawn and Josh to the Gilberts'. They all knew better than to arrive late for one of Aunt Vicki's meals. At least she had been able to bring a good report of the wounded man's condition.

"He's young and healthy," Barbara Newhouse told them during the drive across town. "He responded well to transfusions. Actually, he is suffering more from the embarrassment of shooting himself in the leg than he is from the pain of his injury."

"What was he doing in the Chrystal woods in the middle of the night?" Dawn asked. "That's a silly time to go hunting."

"Rabbits," her mother reminded her, "feed at night."

Josh said nothing. But he hadn't said much since their trip to the hospital early Sunday morning. Not being able to talk to Chelsea was really driving him crazy. He was barely inside the door of the Gilbert house before asking to use the phone. He came back more long-faced than ever.

"Did you reach Chelsea?" Dawn asked, when they had a private minute.

He shook his head. "She's not taking calls," he quoted. "Whatever that means."

"You'll see her at school tomorrow," Dawn reminded him. "Then you'll see that she's all right."

Aunt Vicki's voice pressed in on Dawn again. "I certainly hope you don't expect your respectable friends to visit you in that neighborhood," she was saying. Dawn had a few choice replies she could have made to that remark, but she swallowed them for her mother's sake.

Chelsea's mother had made the decision about no incoming calls. From the moment they awakened that Sunday morning, the phone had rung steadily. Every time it rang, it seemed to vibrate through Chelsea's brain. She felt awful, anyway, even without that noise. She hadn't been able to get back to sleep after the ambulance took the wounded hunter away. Her encounter with the bearded man had haunted her until morning finally came. The last straw had been to discover that the clothing she had put in her car was gone. She inquired, as casually as possible, if Zacchary or Ben had unloaded her car. When both men denied even going near it after putting it away, she felt that terrifying weakness in her legs again.

The bearded man had been there. Somehow he had gotten onto the place, into the garage, and taken the clothing away without anyone noticing him. If he could do that, he could do anything he wanted. His words came back.

"People get killed all the time," he had said in that level tone. "Cars explode when they are started. A big house like the one you live in would go up like a torch if someone fired it."

With his words ringing in her ears, she passed through the hall in time to hear her mother's voice raised in irritation as the phone jangled again.

"Enough is enough," Elizabeth Chrystal

said. "Listen to that. We haven't had a moment's quiet this morning. Let people get their news over tv and radio. This family deserves a little rest."

The phone still rang, of course, but the maid answered it. No matter who called, her response was the same. "The Chrystal family is receiving no calls today." Her mother was right about tv and radio. The item about the wounded hunter got top billing on every newscast, pushed there, of course, by the fact that it had happened on Chrystal land.

All through that strange, terrifying Sunday, Chelsea worked toward getting the money the bearded man had demanded. By nightfall, she was finally ready. She had collected all her own gold jewelry, a lot of Amy's, and some sterling silver pieces that the family seldom used. With what she had in her savings account, she had a good start. She wouldn't really know how close she was until she got to a dealer in precious metals. Every time the phone rang, she cringed, hoping it wasn't the bearded man. What would he do when he wasn't able to reach her? Would he think she was avoiding him and fulfill his threats against the family?

Josh insisted on leaving ridiculously early for school that next day. Dawn would have complained except that she realized how frantic he was to see Chelsea. Besides, being there early might give her a few extra minutes with Pete Carter. Usually Pete waited out front for her with Karen Pickett and her boyfriend Mitch. Today she would fool them and be waiting for *them*!

Dawn watched Pete climb out of Mitch's red car and walk toward the school steps with Karen and Mitch following. Her heart sank at his dark, unsmiling expression.

When he reached her, he didn't even take her hand. Instead he scowled and spoke grimly. "I guess you heard about the new Chrystal horror," he said.

"My mother treated the man at the hospital," she told him. "He's doing fine."

"No thanks to your friends the Chrystals."

"Listen, Pete," she said, looping her arm in his. "Let's make a deal that we leave that one alone. This isn't a Mill-versus-Hill problem. The man was trespassing and he shot himself."

Mitch, behind them, chuckled. "All my life I've heard about people shooting themselves in their own legs. Finally it happened. And Dawn's right, Pete. The guy had no business there. Incidentally, you do remember what's going on today, don't you?"

Dawn looked around, puzzled. Then at Karen's expression, she laughed. "Of course, the volleyball match. Fabulous!"

Karen's lively face flushed with color. As a milltown girl, she was as defensive about Chrystal Falls and its vicious social prejudices as Pete was. But Dawn had been stubborn enough to establish a delicate friendship with this attractive girl who was the best athlete Dawn had ever seen. "Go for it, Karen," Dawn

34

said warmly, which sent the color into Karen's cheeks again.

Once Pete arrived, Dawn forgot Josh was still out there waiting and went inside with Pete. They were starting down the hall when the warning bell pealed. Josh stuck his head in the door, his face tight with concern.

"You do think Chelsea's coming, don't you?" he asked Dawn.

"She had better," Dawn assured him. "If we don't finish that student project between classes today, we'll have to do it tonight."

He nodded, as if her words reassured him, and he went outside again. Within seconds the final bell sounded and Dawn sped for her class. Glancing back, she saw Josh come in the door alone and wished she had time to speak to him again. Chelsea either wasn't coming, or she was late.

The answer was late. The roll had already been taken when Chelsea came into class. She was wearing a backpack Dawn hadn't seen her use before. When she stopped at the desk, the teacher marked in his book, frowning. Chelsea, dark circles under her eyes, with her lovely face ashen, sat down beside her friend Perky Palmer without greeting anyone.

Conscious of Pete so close in the seat behind her, Dawn didn't look around. She didn't need to hear any remarks about Chelsea looking the worse for wear, not even from Pete. It was strange to feel sorry for Chelsea, but suddenly she did.

The day, badly begun, got steadily worse.

At lunchtime Chelsea simply failed to appear. Her little group of Hill girls kept watching the door, as Josh did. Sitting across the room with Pete, Dawn finally motioned him to join them.

Mistake number seven hundred and fifty seven. Either Pete didn't realize how involved Josh was with Chelsea or he didn't care.

Josh was so openly watching the door that Pete finally said, "If you're worried about Chelsea Chrystal, save your energy. The Chrystals have proved again that they can take care of themselves, even if it means setting up an armed camp."

"Hey," Josh said, glaring at him. "How would you like to know some ex-convict was out to get you?"

Pete laughed. "All of us at milltown know who's out to get us. That's nothing new. As for Bill Gurney, he has to know better than to come back here where all the law is Chrystal clear."

"You can just lay off that," Josh said, rising.

Pete rose, too, facing him across the table, his expression challenging. "You want to make me?"

"Josh," Dawn cried, hoping to reason with him. He didn't reply. He just stared at her as angrily as he had at Pete and stalked away, leaving his lunch practically untouched. A buzz of excited whispers hummed from the table where Perky and Chelsea's other friends had been watching.

Pete sat down again without meeting Dawn's eyes. "Listen, Newhouse," he said. "It's no go, pretending we can ignore what's going on up on the Hill. And it's no go between us when you try to stand on both sides of the street. Oil and water, that's us. Never mind the jokes about shooting your own foot. That place was wired and the guard who went after the kid was carrying a gun."

Dawn stared at him. "But he's not a guard, he's just a stable helper."

His smile was twisted as he rose and looked down at her. "Sure, Newhouse. And I'm the King of Siam."

Dawn looked down at her untouched lunch a moment, before carrying it to the disposal bin and throwing the whole thing away. As she passed Perky's table, she heard that cool laughter. "And they're cheaper than a floor show, too," she was saying.

A dull pain always came in her chest when she and Pete had one of these breakups. But this had been so sudden, so cruel. The rest of that day she moved woodenly from one class to another, not meeting anyone's eyes, not caring who saw her pain. Josh had done it, her own brother! If only I'd ignored Pete . . . not argued with him.

Chelsea was in Dawn's last class. If anything, she looked worse than she had first period. Her eyes, always bright, seemed unnaturally brilliant. Dawn leaned to ask about getting together for the project after school.

Chelsea shook her head furiously. "I can't make it," she said. Then she sighed. "How about my place after dinner?"

Leaning back, Dawn saw Karen Pickett watching them, looking amused. As Dawn walked out, Karen fell into step beside her.

"Fasten your seat belt," she warned. "When Chelsea sparkles like that, trouble's on its way for somebody."

Dawn sighed, torn as always between her friendship with Karen and her loyalty to Chelsea. "There's going to be trouble enough if we don't get that student council project finished tonight. It's due in the office first thing tomorrow."

Karen rolled her eyes upward. "I'll send you a sympathy card."

Down the hall Dawn saw Pete Carter moving away without a backward look. Now, she thought miserably. Send me a sympathy card now. It can't feel much worse than this to be dead.

Dawn was surprised to have that evening at the Chrystals start pleasantly enough. Since Amy was watching tv in the family room and her parents were in their sitting room upstairs, Chelsea suggested they lay the project out on the huge dining room table. Chelsea was a little absentminded, having to be reminded of things as they went along, but they were almost through when the phone rang.

Chelsea stepped around the corner into the

kitchen and answered it with her usual lively, "Hello."

After a moment of silence, Chelsea spoke again, her voice low and a little trembly. Dawn didn't hear much of what she was saying, but in a minute Chelsea was back.

"Listen, Dawn," she said swiftly. "I have to go out for a minute. Wait right there; I'll be back."

Dawn started to protest that she could finish it alone, but Chelsea, picking up the backpack, shook her head. "Just wait. This is something I need to deal with, once and for all."

With that she was gone, leaving Dawn staring after her.

Chapter Five

Chelsea stood silently in the darkened kitchen for a long moment. Her heart was thundering so loudly that she feared Dawn could hear it from the next room.

Plan. She must plan.

The caller on the phone hadn't had to tell her who he was. That gravelly voice had flooded her with terror the moment he spoke. She could see him as clearly as if he stood in the dark corner of the room.

"Now I'm ready," he said. "You know the cabin on the ridge, the one the hunters use?"

He had barely paused for her mumbled reply.

"Thirty minutes," he told her. "You got thirty minutes to get there. Alone," he added ominously. "Got that?"

"But it's dark," she protested. "There's no road."

"There's horses," he pointed out. Then he laughed without humor. "There's other ways to deal with the Chrystals if this is too much for you."

His tone was sneering. Other ways.

"I'll be there," she whispered. A moment of silence followed, before she heard the click of the phone being hung up.

Dawn looked up as Chelsea stood in the door of the dining room. Calm, Chelsea told herself sternly. You have to sound calm.

"Listen, Dawn," she said carefully. "I have to go out for a minute. Wait right there; I'll be back."

Dawn's look of astonishment was followed by quick protest. "We're almost through, Chelsea," she began.

From the moment the bearded man had said "thirty minutes" Chelsea had felt the seconds ticking away. Pressed by her terror and the need to hurry, she lifted the backpack loaded with the money and the unsold silver and broke in. "Just wait," she insisted. "This is something I need to deal with, once and for all."

Getting a horse from the stable was the next hurdle. She had to tell someone she was taking a horse out. If she didn't, she would be heard and followed. She hesitated in the stable yard a long moment. The faint hum of Zacchary's tv came from behind his closed door. No. She wouldn't speak to him. He was a strange, silent man who hardly ever smiled, not even at Amy, who could win a smile from anyone. She had a better chance of fooling Ben, whom she had known forever.

She rapped on Ben's door and heard him slowly move across the wooden floor inside. She blazed with impatience until he unchained his door and finally stood there against the light. She grinned up at him as disarmingly as she could. "I have to ride up the hill a ways," she told him. "I left some stuff up there I need for my homework. I'll take Cookie and be right back."

He hesitated, frowning. "It's dark, Miss Chelsea, and coming on rain. Let me go for you. Or at least ride along."

She shook her head, managing a convincing laugh. "Why should we both get drenched? I've ridden these woods all my life. I'll be back before you know it."

He would have argued but she gave him no time. With Cookie swiftly saddled, she rode off, waving at him cheerily. He stood looking after her, under the circle of light from the stable lamps. She rode sedately until she was out of his view, then laid the crop to the mare's hip sharply.

"Go, Cookie, go," she whispered, crouching onto the animal's neck. Already the first splatters of rain had begun, a drumming sound that filled the woods around her. She had chosen Cookie for her surefootedness on the mountain trails. The horse whinnied and shied when the first distant roll of thunder sounded beyond the hill. "Good girl," Chelsea called to her. "Go."

Pressed against Cookie's warm neck, Chelsea felt the backpack bouncing against her spine. She didn't have enough money. Even with her savings account cleaned out and the gold chains all sold, she had managed to raise a little less than four thousand dollars. What would he do? He would have to take the silver serving pieces away from Chrystal Falls to sell them. The smith had recognized the massive teapot and launched into a long story about mending it and how long it had been in the Chrystal family. Afraid to ask him for a price, she had left it with him to be polished. But the flatware, so heavy in the backpack, was worth more than the difference if he would only sell it himself.

What had begun as a few scattered drops became a downpour as she pressed the horse nearer to the top of the ridge. Rivulets of water were already coursing down the narrow trail. Cookie slid and almost stumbled on the wet clay before Chelsea finally eased up with her crop.

"A half hour is a long time," she told herself.

Why was she trying to fool herself? A half hour went very fast, and what would he do when he found she had not brought enough money?

The stable lights had blinded her at first, forcing her to depend on the horse's familiarity with the path. By the time she neared the hunter's cabin, her eyes had adjusted to the rain-slick woods. The wind had risen, whipping the trees wildly as the thunder sounded steadily nearer.

She fought hysteria as the horse strained the last few yards of the hill. How had she gotten into this? Was she doing the right thing? Would he go away now and not hurt the people she loved? The reins were sodden in her grasp and little streams dripped from her hair, flooding her neck with icy water.

Would the money be enough?

Then she was at the edge of the clearing. A faint flickering of lightning, very far away, lit the cabin for a split second. Her heart sank. No one was there. Had he tricked her? She held her breath. She heard nothing except the whine of the wind in the trees and the distant mutter of thunder. Sliding from Cookie's back, she tied the reins around a sapling and started toward the cabin. Just forcing her legs to walk toward the place took all her strength. She cried without meaning to, her tears mingling with the steady, cold rain.

The door stood open but she couldn't make herself step inside. Instead, she paused on the rotting stoop, listening. Something rustled from the woods beyond, sending a shiver up her spine. Far off, somewhere, a dog howled mournfully. From the inside of the cabin came no sound at all.

"Hello?" she called softly.

At that moment she almost turned and ran.

She saw nothing but darkness beyond the door of the cabin. She could hear nothing but the drumming of the rain on the cabin roof. A musty, earthy smell filled her head. He wasn't there. He couldn't be or she would be able to sense it.

It all happened at once, too quickly. Something slammed against her, hard, throwing her against the side of the door. She heard a hollow, sickening sound as her skull smashed against the wood, sending a searing pain blazing down her body.

The door. It registered that the door must have swung against her, knocking her off her feet. She clung to the wall. If she could only get back onto her feet, she was sure she could steady her reeling head. But even as the waves of blackness shuddered through her consciousness, the room seemed to explode around her. At first she thought lightning had struck a tree near the clearing. The noise was that loud and vibrating. In its aftermath, her ears throbbed with a sick, echoing rhythm. But a swift light came with that explosion of sound, not the jagged brilliance of lightning but a hot, sudden light, there and gone in an instant. A fresh pain was added to her agony. Her hand hurt as painfully as if it had been caught in a slammed door. She tried to scream, even knowing there was no one there to hear. Only a moan sounded as she clawed at the wall, trying to rise.

Nothing made sense, not the sudden pain in her hand, not the dark shadow appearing fleetingly on the wall above her head. Not the darkness that filled the room and then her mind as she moaned helplessly, "No, no, no."

Dawn's first reaction to Chelsea's departure was annoyance. "But Chelsea," she called after her friend. It was too late. She heard the back door close even as she spoke.

"Oh," she groaned in irritation. If she had only brought the car, she would just leave. Since she had to wait for Josh to come pick her up, she might as well finish the project.

Later she had no idea how long she had worked there in silence. It couldn't have been more than a few minutes before she heard the tapping of a cane in the hall and looked up to see Chelsea's grandmother in the doorway. The old woman had obviously dressed in haste. Her usually immaculate hair was all messed up. She looked terribly frail and frightened.

"Chelsea?" she asked. "Where's Chelsea?"

Dawn had risen as Mrs. Chrystal entered.

"Was that Chelsea on the phone?" Mrs. Chrystal went on without waiting for answers.

At Dawn's nod, Mrs. Chrystal turned pale and groped for a chair. "Listen, my dear," she said, her voice rattled with urgency. "Run upstairs as fast as you can go. Get Alexander. Tell him to hurry. Run, now, run!"

Alexander Chrystal, wearing a dark velvet jacket, came to the door at Dawn's first knock. He nodded at her message and crossed the hall instantly. Chelsea's mother was right behind him, the heels of her mules slapping a little on the stairs.

Amy came out of the family room as Dawn went by. "What's up?" she asked.

Before Dawn could answer, Mr. Chrystal was calling her imperiously from the dining room. Lillian Chrystal, her head in her hands, was weeping. "I should have called the minute I heard that conversation," she said. "It didn't sound like Chelsea's voice. I thought at first it might be one of the maids."

"Never mind that," her son said sternly. "Repeat the words exactly."

"He said he was ready," Mrs. Chrystal reported. "Then something about her only having thirty minutes."

"Where?" her son asked. "Where?"

"The cabin on the ridge," the old woman repeated. "The one the hunters use."

She had barely finished before he turned to Amy and Dawn. "You girls, get to the stable. Have horses saddled. Hurry now." He turned from them to reach for the phone.

Everything happened too swiftly after that. Mr. Chrystal, with a down vest over his velvet jacket, was swinging onto his horse, giving orders to Ben. "I've called the police," he said. "Lead them in." Then he saw Amy with her pony. "What are you doing, Amy? Stay here with your mother."

Amy swung into the saddle, extending a hand down for Dawn. "We're coming, Dad," she said firmly. "She's our Chelsea, too."

Startled by her tone, he looked at her

steadily, then shrugged. Zacchary, on the bay stallion, was already crossing the yard toward the wood. "Very well, but hurry!"

Dawn clung to Amy's slender body. She hadn't been crazy about riding since she'd had a terrible horseback riding accident that had left her ill for a long time. The sweep of the tree limbs past their heads terrified her, bringing back those awful weeks of amnesia. Even if she had liked riding, she wouldn't have enjoyed that night. Rain pelted them as the horse pressed up the hill. Every few minutes the sky was split by jagged chasms of lightning followed by crashes of thunder. Up ahead the men's horses snorted as they were goaded into the storm.

"Who was it? Who called?" Amy shouted back at Dawn.

"I don't know," Dawn admitted, tightening her hold on the child's waist. "She just left."

The ground leveled a bit as they approached the clearing. "Thank God," she heard Alexander Chrystal say. "We're almost there."

His words were lost in a sudden explosion of sound. Gunfire. Amy cried out, kicking her pony hard. "Chelsea," she cried, sudden tears in her voice. "Chelsea."

When they broke into the clearing, the men were already half off their horses. Amy and Dawn were right behind them as they approached the door of the cabin. Zacchary was carrying a cocked gun and a broad-beamed flashlight.

The fan of light from Zacchary's lantern

48

spread on the sill of the open door. Chelsea was on her knees just inside the door, her head drooped at an odd angle. Her eyes were open but she didn't seem to be seeing. The air smelled like the Fourth of July. As Dawn stood there, frozen, she saw Chelsea slump over and fall awkwardly onto the littered floor. As she did, something clattered from her hand. Amy, at Dawn's side, gasped and grabbed Dawn's arm, clutching her tightly. The gun was short and thick, with a snub nose. It shone blue in the steady gleam of the flashlight.

"Chelsea," Mr. Chrystal cried in an anguished tone, leaning toward his daughter.

Zacchary spoke up quickly. "You better not touch anything," he warned. As he spoke he moved the beam of the flashlight toward the rear of the small, leaf-cluttered room. Against the wall, with his chin resting on the widening bloodstain on his chest, slumped a young blond man, his hands outstretched on the floor, palms up.

Through the sound of the rain and the intermittent thunder still grumbling across the mountains came the far, shrill sound of sirens winding their way up the hill.

At the sight of the wounded young man, Amy had twisted around to bury her head against Dawn. Dawn held her close, patting her back, murmuring reassurance. What could she say? They had all heard the gun fire. They had all seen the gun fall from Chelsea's hand, and gasped at the shattered chest of the unconscious man across the room.

The police came on foot, led by Ben. Flash-bulbs exploded while the medics lifted Chelsea to her feet and put the young blond man onto a stretcher. Slipping on the wet path, the medics set off at a swift trot, disappearing at once into the woods as they started down the path toward the road.

A policeman led Chelsea to a car and Dawn supported her on one side. Dawn's head began to ache, to pound with rebellion at the scenes that flashed painfully, one after another, through her brain.

At home, Amy's mother slid the child off the pony into comforting arms. Inside the house Dawn burst into tears to find her Uncle Walt waiting. He held her as tight as she had held Amy, and much the same way. He had been called to see to Grandma Lillian, whose health was not strong enough for such excitement and terror as the past hour had held.

Dawn tried to tell her uncle how strange Chelsea had looked, lying there in the doorway. "Something's awfully wrong with Chelsea, Uncle Walt. Her eyes, and the way she passed out."

"She'll be in good hands," he assured her. "She's been taken to the hospital, and your mother is on duty at Emergency tonight."

The driveway was half filled with cars, a patrol car among them, by the time Josh came to get her. He didn't turn off the motor. Nor did he even knock at the door. He just burst in, his eyes wild, looking around desperately.

"What's going on?" he asked, seeing his Uncle Walt. "What in the world is going on?"

Dawn couldn't answer. She only shook her head and fought back her tears.

"Nobody really knows yet," Uncle Walt told Josh.

"Then why are they saying over the radio that Chelsea Chrystal is the suspect in an attempted murder?" Josh challenged him.

Murder. Until that moment Dawn had seen the events happen like a series of pictures flashed before her eyes. That word gave the pictures a new and hideous shape. Murder.

She dropped onto the divan and began to cry helplessly.

Chapter Six

For nineteen hours the medical team at Chrystal Falls Memorial Hospital fought for the life of the young blond man found in the hunter's cabin. In spite of their desperate efforts, they were unable even to bring him back to consciousness. By the time he died that Tuesday afternoon at three o'clock, the police had identified him as Ralph Schroeder.

A young man of twenty-three who had originally come from West Virginia, Schroeder had left the state penitentiary only two weeks before. He had completed a five-year term for armed robbery and assault with a deadly weapon. His history of juvenile crime dated from the age of thirteen, when he had been one of a gang of youngsters convicted of beating up an aging peddler in a robbery attempt. He was single, survived only by a widowed mother, still a resident of West Virginia.

Dawn Newhouse, unable to shake the headache that had started on the way down the hill from the hunting cabin, lay with a wet wash-cloth on her forehead, staring at the ceiling of her room. The events of that Tuesday had overwhelmed her. As much television as she had watched in her life, Dawn thought she had a pretty accurate idea of how the law worked. She was astonished that the grand jury had convened early in the morning of the day after the shooting.

The grand jury itself amazed her. She hadn't realized how many people would be summoned for that private and secret hearing. While her mother was still working along with the rest of the emergency team trying to save Ralph Schroeder's life, Dawn was served with a subpoena and called to testify. Chelsea was not there. That made sense, of course, because Chelsea was in the hospital being treated for a severe concussion, multiple abrasions, and a badly bruised right hand. Still, it was amazing that no one appeared on Chelsea's behalf to question Dawn's testimony.

In her wildest nightmares she could not have imagined how horrifying it would be to stand before that panel of unsmiling, curious people and answer their questions under oath. Only when she heard her own answers and saw the reactions on the faces of the jury members did she grasp how damaging her words were to Chelsea Chrystal.

The hardest moment came when the prose-cutor demanded that she repeat the last words Chelsea Chrystal had said to her, when she left Dawn in the dining room of the Chrystal home.

Dawn remembered the words all too well. "This is something I need to deal with, once and for all."

"Where was the gun when you first went to the door of the hunter's shack?"

"In Chelsea Chrystal's hand."

"What else did you see in that room?"

Describing the wounded man had been the worst, because the moment she began to tell them what she saw, the scene in the cabin came back vividly to her mind. She saw the blond man just the way he had been, slumped over, his weaponless hands spread out, the blood spot widening on his shirt.

Dawn was finally sent out by the magistrate to wait in an outside room, in case they had further questions for her. As she left the room she passed Zacchary being led in to give his testimony.

Even though the grand jury itself met in secret, there was no rule against witnesses talking to people after they left the room. From the conversations of those around her, Dawn began to see the evidence against Chelsea as a mountain rising to smother all of them.

Every word of testimony, every piece of evidence seemed to tighten a noose of guilt around Chelsea. The shirt the dead man wore had been Monty Chrystal's, monogrammed with his initials. The gold watch in the dead man's pocket, its strap shattered by the passing bullet, was inscribed "To C.C. from L.C. with love at Christmas." Although the backpack Chelsea claimed to have carried to the cabin was not found, its contents as she described them were strewn around the dying man: almost four thousand dollars in cash, a number of articles of clothing from the Chrystal home, and an eighteenth-century silver teapot from the family collection along with a quantity of sterling flatware.

When Dawn had finally been dismissed to go home, Josh was waiting. His face, beside her in the car, looked as if it had been turned to stone. He didn't ask her what had gone on inside the courthouse.

"Whatever you do, don't turn on the radio or watch tv when we get home," he warned her. "It's pure torture."

She nodded silently. After the torture just past, she never wanted to hear another word about the events in the cabin. She never wanted to have another curious face staring back at her. Curious faces. Remembering the reaction of the kids at school, she shuddered.

"School tomorrow," she said. "Josh, I can't deal with it. Surely Mom will relent and let me stay home?"

He shook his head. "You've got to take the plunge someday."

"Bath of fire," she told him.

He nodded. "Maybe we could stay all the way out of it, keep from being involved."

She groaned. "Josh, how can I be uninvolved when I had to stand in there as a witness? Anyway, in this town, anyone who doesn't take the Mill side or the Hill side is going to get killed in the crossfire."

The tv and the radio weren't the only things they had to avoid. The rack at the store where they stopped for milk held a stack of late editions with four-inch headlines. HEIRESS SHOWERED MURDERED EX-CON LOVER WITH GIFTS AND MONEY.

The picture was the one that had been taken the day Chelsea dedicated the new shopping center. They had run an old picture of the dead man, taken in his teens. In the picture he looked nothing like the wounded man in the cabin. Instead he looked young and handsome enough to make it believable that the beautiful, smiling young Chelsea really might have been attracted to him.

Naturally Aunt Vicki had to rush in where television news people were not allowed to tread. Dawn heard the phone and the rumble of Josh's voice from the other room. He came back slowly and dropped onto the divan next to her. After a minute, he stretched and flipped off the lamp. They sat a moment in the darkness before he could get his voice to work.

"Aunt Vicki," he said. "She couldn't wait for us to find out that the grand jury decision has been announced. They have indicted Chelsea for the murder of Ralph Schroeder."

Dawn couldn't speak. She could hardly breathe. Finally she asked, "What does that mean, Josh?"

56

"According to our helpful aunt it means that Chelsea will be put under arrest."

"But she's in the hospital," Dawn protested.

"They'll post guards, and a date will be set for the arraignment. That's when she will plead guilty or not guilty."

"She's not guilty," Dawn said hotly.

"I'm as sure of that as you are," Josh replied. "But pleading not guilty means she'll have to go to trial."

"But what about the meantime?"

Josh shrugged. "Surely the judge will set a bond so she won't have to go to jail until the trial date."

"I don't know how they can possibly have believed she would murder anyone!" Dawn wailed.

"The gun was registered to the Chrystal Mills. The manager claimed that no one remembered seeing it for years, but nobody had reported it missing."

Dawn reached for Josh's hand in the dark. When she found it, he gripped her fingers so hard that she almost cried out.

Chelsea's father was with her when the police investigators came to interrogate her about the events of that Monday night. They sent the nurse away and tried to insist that her father leave, too, but he was able to talk them into letting him stay.

It seemed unreal that she was answering the questions she had heard so many times on tv and in movies. Her father referred to them as

57

the "Miranda" questions. They explained her rights to speak or remain silent. She nodded, her eyes on her father's face.

Later she was almost sorry he was there. She wanted to tell them the story the way it happened, but they wouldn't have it that way.

First they asked about the dead man. That was what they called him. "When did you first meet the dead man, Ralph Schroeder?"

"I never met him. I never saw him before in my life."

They looked at each other and then asked about the things she had taken to the cabin.

"They weren't for him. They were for the bearded man who threatened me on the road."

In the end, they let her tell the story as it happened. She couldn't even glance at her father's face when she explained why she had made the decision to get the money for him. They recorded everything she said, but their faces told her they thought she was lying.

Three separate times they asked her to tell exactly what happened when she stepped into the cabin. The third time the policeman didn't even let her finish. Instead, he just sighed and turned off the recorder. "This is getting us nowhere," he told his companion.

"What's going to happen?" she asked her father when they had left. "I never saw that man in my life. I know I didn't kill him."

Her father leaned to kiss her. He smelled of the spicy after-shave lotion he always wore. She reached up to hug him but her arms hurt too much. He held her lightly. "Try to sleep, love," he told her. "And don't worry."

Even when she drifted off, the pain wakened her. Flowers kept coming and the nurse read the cards to her. The Simpson family, Perky Palmer and her folks, Maggie Janko and her father, everybody at the club. Then, while dinner was being served, a little pot of pale blue African violets came. "There isn't any signature," the nurse said. "It only says, 'Hang in there,' followed by the letter M."

The pot was small enough to fit on her bed-side table. Who did she know with the initial M who would think of something so delicate, so comforting? Her brother Monty had the initial M, but he would never think of anything tender like sending her violets.

The crossfire Dawn had dreaded at school started at the front door. First, of course, they had to take aim. Every kid in the hall stared as she walked toward her locker. Excited conversations stopped in the middle of sentences when she walked by. Ryan Simpson, deep in conversation with Perky Palmer, stared at her thoughtfully as she passed.

Dawn could almost see the wheels turn behind Ryan's forehead. He said something to Perky, then called out to her. "Dawn. Wait up."

Dawn stared at him. Ryan had barely acknowledged her existence in the whole time they had lived there. After Josh knocked him out of the coveted first singles position on the tennis team, he had made it clear that the Newhouse family was nowhere for him. When Chelsea, who had always been Ryan's girl, became an item with Josh Newhouse, the real ice age had set in.

In step behind her, Ryan looked intently into her face. He had the greedy look of someone excited and hungry. "What happened?" he asked. "What really happened up there? What did you see?"

"I can't talk about it," Dawn managed to say, disgusted at his sick curiosity.

Ryan frowned thoughtfully. "Oh," he said. "Because of the trial and all. Don't worry. The prosecuting attorney used to be a member of the Chrystal firm."

The Chrystal firm. Dawn stopped in her tracks so quickly that someone bumped into her as she started after Ryan. That would be the law firm of Chrystal, Palmer, and whatever. Did the Hill kids really think this was something that could be handled with family connections? What had Pete said that made Josh so furious? "The law is Chrystal clear?"

"Hey," someone called angrily behind her, "watch what you're doing."

She turned to face one of the milltown boys whose name she didn't know. His expression was mocking. "I guess you *all* think you can get away with murder," he said, as he passed on down the hall.

She wasn't ready for that. She fled into the

rest room to see Perky Palmer preening before the mirror.

"What a shock," Perky said. "Your brother must be blown away by all this. Who would have thought Chelsea would have a secret love off on the side?"

Dawn, stunned, did not register that Karen Pickett was there. Karen, her dark eyes flashing, walked to the basin beside Perky and deliberately turned the water on hard enough to splash over the bowl.

"Why not?" she challenged Perky. "It was good enough for you, wasn't it?"

Perky's mouth dropped for only a single moment before her face flamed with color. She wiped the front of her dress with her hand and turned to leave. At the door she stopped and spat back at Karen, almost like a cat. "Trash!" she said. "Milltown trash!"

Dawn breathed out slowly. Perky had asked for it. The hit-and-run accident that almost killed Amy Chrystal's little friend Miles had happened when Perky had sneaked out with a forbidden boy who had stolen Mitch's car. If the child had not come out of his coma and been able to talk, Karen's boyfriend Mitch would have been tried for manslaughter.

"It takes one to know one," Karen said bitterly. Then she frowned soberly at Dawn. "Boy, do you have a knack of being at all the wrong places! But don't fret, they'll never kill a Chrystal, not even for murder!"

"Karen," Dawn pleaded. "Don't say that.

Chelsea didn't kill anybody. I don't care what it looks like now. She didn't. She couldn't."

Karen shook her head. "Slow learner, Newhouse. Don't lay any bets on it."

Karen, with her arm linked with Mitch's, was only a few steps ahead of Dawn as she walked dully down the hall toward class. Mitch glanced back, looked as if he had something to say, then turned away.

Dawn paused at the door of the English room, looking around for an empty seat. Pete Carter was already at his usual place by the window. Just the sight of him made that drumming pain in her head suddenly worse. He glanced toward the door, his eyes passing over her as if she were invisible. Mr. Elkins was talking to another teacher. Dawn didn't mean to eavesdrop, but his voice, rich with unaccustomed laughter, carried too well.

"She's certainly never been that creative in this class!" he said. "A bearded man on a lonely road. Rather a nice touch for a B student."

Somehow Dawn made it to an empty chair.

Chapter Seven

As the bell jangled, Dawn's classmates scraped to their feet and moved in an almost solid mass toward the door. Pete Carter seemed to have a separate space of his own. Tall, almost arrogantly straight, he shoved the heavy chairs aside to make himself a private aisle. That way he could follow the crowd out without meeting Dawn's eyes.

Only when Dawn glanced up to see Mr. Elkins watching her did she rise to leave. His expression was amused and somehow triumphant. Why did this man despise the Chrystals so much? Why was everyone so delighted to see a Chrystal in trouble? Wasn't it enough that the family had been publicly disgraced when Monty burned the garden house and then made that terrifying attack on her? What was it going to take to satisfy Chrystal Falls?

Dawn didn't even glance up as she turned into the hall. She didn't notice Ryan Simpson leaning against the wall until he called her name and fell into step beside her. "Listen, Dawn," he began.

"I don't have to listen," she told him. "I don't have any juicy gossip to satisfy your filthy curiosity, and anyway, I heard you before. I know what you think."

He caught her arm so firmly that she glanced up in surprise. His eyes were sober on hers and his expression intense. "What makes you such a know-it-all, Dawn Newhouse? Sure, I'm curious. Why wouldn't I be? Chelsea and I are hardly strangers, you know. As to knowing what I think, haven't you ever heard of anyone whistling in the dark?"

She stared at him, puzzled both by his words and by the concern in his face. "Hey," he went on. "I was asking you what happened up there because I wanted to hear some good news for a change. All I want is to get this whole thing explained and over for Chelsea."

"But what you said about the prosecuting attorney, that was true, wasn't it?"

"*Was* is right," he said bitterly, letting go of her arm. As they walked along, he kept in step with her with his light, athletic stride. With his head down like that and half turned away, she couldn't tell if he was being sincere or just trying to lure her into talking to him about Chelsea.

"It was true until the grand jury indicted Chelsea," he said. "Randy Killam resigned from the case before he got asked to. The state attorney has already sent in another man."

Ryan glanced at her. "According to Perky Palmer's dad, this man they've sent in is a real hawk, vulture maybe. He's got his eye on the governor's chair. He'll see to it that this case is splashed all over the state even if it means he has to kill Chelsea in the process."

Dawn turned to him, tears suddenly hot behind her eyes. "That's not fair, Ryan. He can't do that to Chelsea."

He shrugged. "Let's hope you're right." Then he smiled, his expression suddenly shy. "I know we've never been friends, Dawn, but right now I think Chelsea's friends ought to stick together."

Dawn, looking up at him, wished she could believe his words were sincere. She knew more *about* him than she knew *him*. This was Ryan with the fancy car, the private indoor swimming pool, as much a Hill kid as you could get without being born a Chrystal. Still, for that one moment, he had looked almost as pained as Josh had looked when he heard about the shooting up in the cabin. For a swift moment she was tempted to accept his words for their face value and give him the kind of reassurance she had tried to give Josh, until he got into that stupid argument with Pete. Then Perky passed and Dawn caught the glance that passed between her and Ryan. She felt as if her veins had suddenly been flooded with ice water.

Turning blindly, Dawn started for the dressing room through the rush of girls hurrying to change. Karen Pickett was among them but she stopped and looked back, her eyes sweeping over Ryan with disdain. Without even looking back at Ryan, Dawn followed Karen through the door. Whatever Karen said was lost in the deafening noise of eager players warming up for the game.

The nausea that had begun with her English teacher's taunting words about Chelsea had settled in the pit of Dawn's stomach. She breathed deeply as she tugged at her tennis-shoe laces. If only her feelings would show in a tangible enough way that the school nurse would excuse her. If she could only force her temperature to rise a couple of degrees or lose her voice with laryngitis. Sick at heart was never going to pass muster at the infirmary.

Karen, beside her, dressed in brisk, angry movements. "Simp the wimp looked a little hang-dog out there. I bet that's some kind of act he's staging for you. He's not above putting on a pity-party to try to get some dirt out of you about Chelsea."

"Maybe he cares," Dawn told her. Even though she secretly agreed with Karen, she was annoyed at the scathing hatred in her voice. "Knowing how this crummy town takes sides, he really could be worried about every jackal coming in for the kill."

Karen paused to stare at her. "A man is dead, Newhouse, and Chelsea killed him. Doesn't even that take the glitter off the princess for you? You were there, weren't you, saw the smoking gun and all that?"

"The gun wasn't smoking," Dawn corrected

her. "Even if Chelsea had it in her hand, I don't believe she fired it. I simply don't believe it."

Karen pulled the corners of her mouth down and forced her locker door shut. "Surely you read the papers. They found gunpowder stains on her right hand. I guess those flew across the room from the dying man and glued themselves to her lily-white hands."

Karen's tone was pointlessly acid. Dawn looked at her and shook her head. "You and Pete," she said disgustedly.

Karen flushed. "It's not just me and Pete, Newhouse. It's everybody who can't buy their way into that charmed circle. We know that Hill bunch. The question is not whether they will manage to clear Chelsea, only when they will get it done. Nobody cares a hoot about the dead man except his mother."

Her words caught Dawn off-guard. "Mother?" she echoed lamely.

Karen jerked her combination lock down viciously. "Yeah, mother, just like yours and mine. Only that poor old lady is scared of her shadow, a little farm type trying to deal with a dead son under the glare of television cameras. And all this time, Miss Princess of Chrystal Falls is lolling in a hospital bed wearing something tasteful in imported silk and pretending she's too sick to go to jail."

"She does have a concussion, Karen," Dawn reminded her.

Karen shook her head. "What a sucker you are, Newhouse. If your head was as big as your heart, you'd have to haul it around in a wheelbarrow. Chelsea Chrystal will come out of this smelling like a rose. That girl never changes. Mark that!"

Karen turned and ran out onto the gym floor. Dawn stared after her, drawing a deep, painful breath past that heavy place in her chest. How could anyone as bright as Karen be so pigheaded when it came to the rivalry in the town? But then, Pete was no dummy, either, and he was the same way. It was almost as if the smoke from the mills had poisoned their minds. But what had poisoned the minds of the Hill kids? The coach was calling. Maybe she was glad not to have to try to answer her own question.

Propped on a pile of white pillows, Chelsea watched the hospital attendant set a fresh arrangement of tea roses on the ledge of her windowsill. The flowers were the same clear, pale yellow as the gown and bed jacket her mother's friend Lavinia had sent from New York.

The gown was wonderful, barely a wisp of a top above a huge, swirling skirt. She had never owned anything half as daring. It was just like Lavinia to think of something astonishing to send in the hope of raising her spirits. The jacket was even more exciting than the gown, if possible. It had full, sweeping sleeves trimmed with the same fluttering white ostrich plumes that swayed along the hem.

Any other time she would have danced

wildly in the full-skirted gown and buried her face in the matching tea roses. Instead she sat still and silent, remembering her father's warning that she "must not hurry to appear well."

Chelsea tried not to be conscious of the passing of the days, but everything contrived to remind her. Because of her illness, she had been able to plead "not guilty in absentia," without having to go to court herself. But that was only the beginning according to her father. Now the attorney for the state would be busy interviewing prospective witnesses and getting expert testimony to use against her.

Every day fresh flowers were delivered to her hospital room and the faded bouquets carried away. Her mother, always proper, collected the cards and took them home to write notes to the senders. More than anything Chelsea wanted her mother to settle by the bed, hold her hand, and talk to her about what had happened. Instead Elizabeth Chrystal flitted restlessly from one flower vase to another like a distracted bee.

"You must know who sent these lovely violets," her mother said for about the tenth time, as she lifted the card on the little plant on Chelsea's bedside table.

Chelsea shook her head. "Just don't take the card away," she told her mother. "Maybe it will help me figure out who sent them." She wished she could think it was Josh, because the violets were the warmest, sweetest thing in the whole room. The very thought of Josh brought a thickness to her throat. What was he thinking about all this? Surely he didn't believe all that stuff in the papers and on tv about her having some nasty criminal for a lover. If he missed her, why hadn't he written? Was it because he didn't know what to say, or because he wanted nothing to do with her after all this scandal?

"I don't care what he thinks," she whispered to herself. "I just want him here." The thought of having her head against his chest, with his hands warm against her back, brought tears to her eyes. But no one was allowed to visit except her family, the hospital personnel, and the police.

She had never been so lonely in her life. The women who cleaned the room mumbled a greeting but never met her eyes. Only the mysterious little pot of violets bloomed fresh every day, the flowers like hopeful promises. She counted the blossoms every day. Every time one darkened and withered, a new one sprang up in its place, cool and tender against the touch of her finger.

Not even the carefully controlled visits from her family helped. Even if her mother wasn't so restless when she was there, Chelsea knew Elizabeth Chrystal wouldn't be able to face her. Her mother was too much the lady to let anyone see her eyes hollowed by anguish. It was a matter of both pride and training for her to hide her deepest emotions. Amy sat silent and wide-eyed, clearly trying to think of something to say that didn't touch on the monstrous fact that Chelsea's trial was grinding nearer by the day. On the doctor's counsel, her grandparents were not encouraged to come.

"We must make every effort to abide by the police's rules on your detention," her father explained.

Aside from the tv coverage, her father was her only source of news. He explained why the prosecuting attorney, Randy Killam, whom she had known since she was a child, had withdrawn from the case. The man sent in by the state was "a different sort," her father said. Chelsea saw the man, Bradley J. Larrimore, on the tv news. He was a slender man with a great shock of pale hair and a long, narrow nose that divided his unsmiling face unevenly. Even his name somehow sounded sinister.

Lacking anything better to do, she slept a lot and listened idly to the regular rhythm of the hospital. She quickly learned to recognize the changing of shifts and the approach of mealtime, which was heralded by carts rattling along the hall. Visiting hours were easy enough. When the uniformed guard stepped in, nodded, and pulled her door shut, she knew the hall would soon be full of families and friends, visiting the other patients. Burying her head in her pillow, she tried not to hear the whispers beyond the door and imagine the curious looks the police guard got from everyone who passed.

"Why can't I go home?" she asked her father. "They can't keep me here forever, can they?"

Her father didn't meet her eyes. "We are working on that, Chelsea," he told her. "I have a new attorney who is trying to get bond set."

She stared at him. "What do they think I am, a dangerous criminal or something?"

"Of course not, dear," he said in that soothing tone that he didn't realize was so insulting.

"Then why doesn't the judge set bond?"

He sighed. "You ran away once, you know, that time to New York?"

She wanted to shout at him that that had been different. She hadn't really been running away then. She had taken the only way she could think of to escape from her brother Monty.

She couldn't think of the words *first degree murder* without her heart thundering wildly with terror. She gripped her hands into tight little fists, just trying to keep her emotions under control until he leaned to kiss her good-bye.

Her father had barely left when the nurse entered with a doctor Chelsea had never seen before.

"What's the matter?" she asked, chilled by the man's unsmiling manner.

"Just a little examination," the nurse murmured, her tone soothing.

"But Dr. Walt examined me this morning,"

she protested. "I don't want to be examined by anyone but Dr. Walt or my own doctor." As she spoke, Chelsea pulled the silky jacket closer around her throat.

Only then did the doctor raise his eyes to hers. "Release your gown, Miss Chrystal," he said, his tone icy. "I am not here for your pleasure but by order of the court."

Chelsea felt her heart pounding under the tapping of his fingers, remembering her father's warning about appearing too well. He had only warned her, not told her what would happen if she seemed to be recovered from her injuries. He hadn't had to tell her, she knew. If no bail was set and she was judged well, they could only send her to jail.

At the very word she saw the massive stone structure clearly in her mind, its broad doors grim and forbidding, its windows hidden behind steel bars that reflected the late-afternoon light. But that was unthinkable. They couldn't send her there, not her, not Chelsea Chrystal.

When the nurse came with the tray, Chelsea just sat staring at it for a long time. Then she ate slowly, wondering what cook at home was serving, wondering what they talked about at home during dinner. She missed Amy being loose and relaxed with her. She missed her own room with her favorite records throbbing from the stereo in her alcove. She forced herself to think of familiar places, to keep the dark panic from fluttering in her chest so that her breath came fast and hurting.

Nothing worked. The darkness was out there, beyond the guards at her door, a darkness that nothing could lighten. She heard the evening visiting hours begin and draw to a close. Only when the halls were completely silent again did she lean past the blue violets, flip on the tv across the room, and light up her bedside lamp.

Just having color and sound in the room helped. She picked up the mail her father had left and began to open the cards and read them, glancing only now and then at the tv screen. When the camera shot showed a stout, elderly man descending from an airplane, she paid little attention. That would be some politician, she decided, a statesman off to argue a treaty or something. She was startled to hear the reporter speak her name.

"Attorney for Chelsea Chrystal, awaiting trial for the alleged slaying of Ralph Schroeder," the reporter explained. The reporter, microphone in hand, was running alongside the striding attorney, attempting to get a statement. When the bulky man in the trench coat refused to speak, the reporter's face filled the entire screen. "Jerome Sexton's international notoriety rests on his brilliant defense in sensational murder trials. That Alexander Chrystal has retained Sexton for his daughter's defense is interpreted as indicative of the strength of the state's evidence against the young heiress."

"But I never saw the man in my life," Chelsea whispered to the empty room. Looking down, she realized she had crumpled a pale blue envelope into a wad as she watched. She spread it out on her lap. The envelope bore no return address. Instead of a card, the envelope held a single piece of lined paper.

The message was lettered in an awkward hand. "Hang in there." The only signature was the letter M.

Chelsea tightened both hands on the letter and stared at the blue violets under her lamp. How could this strange message on cheap colored paper be so reassuring? She felt a surge of grateful love for whoever out there cared this much, wanting nothing in return.

She pulled the string on the lamp and turned on the side that didn't hurt. M. She was sure she had thought of everyone she had ever known with the initial M. Who was she missing? Who in her world was she missing?

Chapter Eight

With the door carefully shut to keep her mother from seeing what she was doing, Karen Pickett dumped all the money she owned out on her bedspread. No matter how she counted it, it still came to only seventeen dollars and forty-seven cents. This after saving half her lunch money for two weeks. Her bed looked the way it used to when she emptied her uniform pockets after waiting tables at the Chrystal Falls Country Club. That money had been important because it helped her mother pay bills while her dad was laid off at the mill.

Now, with Mitch's birthday barely a week away, money was important again. What she wouldn't give to have a great pile of money instead of that little one! Not a huge pile but just enough to buy Mitch something he would really love, like a new watch that wouldn't eat quartz batteries every week or so. Or a ring with his initials intertwined on a flat gold surface. He probably wouldn't wear it because of the machinery he worked around, but it would be so great to know he had it.

Shoving the money aside, she sat on her bed with her chin in her hands. According to the newspaper, Chelsea Chrystal had literally showered her ex-con boyfriend with expensive gifts — a cashmere sweater, her own gold watch, and more money than Karen had ever seen. It must be nice, she thought bitterly. If I were Chelsea — She stopped the thought halfway through. No way was she going to think like that. Discovering that Chelsea's father and her own mother had been sweethearts once had nearly blown her away. "I could have been Chelsea Chrystal," she had told herself more than once. Not the same, of course, but rich like Chelsea, rich enough to buy herself a lover. Not that she would ever have been that stupid. And not that she would ever trade her own folks and Mitch for Chelsea's glittery life on the Hill.

Pete. Karen swung her legs off the bed and scooped the money into her jeans pocket. Pete was Mitch's best friend. He would know what Mitch would *really* like for his birthday. She dialed the number at the Carter house and listened to it ring. She was ready to hang up when Pete answered the phone breathlessly. "I just walked in," he told her. "What's up?"

"Mitch's birthday," Karen told him, explaining that she really needed help coming up with something special enough.

"That shouldn't be hard," he said. "Want

to meet me at Mom and Pop's? I need to be over in that part of town, anyway."

"Thirty minutes," Karen told him. "Think hard."

Pete was there before her with the afternoon paper spread out on the table in front of him.

"What's the latest in our Hill scandal?" she asked, taking the bench across from him.

He raised his shoulders at her without looking up. "What a jackal that state's attorney is," he said. "He got the court's permission to send a new doctor in to examine Chelsea. Since the new man is giving her a clean bill of health, the attorney for the state is insisting that she leave the hospital and go to jail."

Karen craned her head to see. TOO GOOD FOR OUR JAIL? the headline asked in bold, two-inch letters. "Why don't they just put up bond?"

"Don't you remember? The judge refused to let her put up bond because murder is a capital crime and she is a proven runaway. Oops," he added. "We missed our chance to plot Mitch's birthday!"

Looking around, Karen felt that wonderful leap of delight that always came when she saw Mitch. His grin as he approached promised them both a good teasing. He caught her thigh with a strong, loving pinch as he slid in beside her. "Who do I beat up on first?" he asked. "My gal or my best friend? Sneaking around behind my back, are you?"

"Sure thing," Pete told him. "You noticed

how we picked a place you didn't know about."

Karen pulled the paper over while they ordered. When she finished reading the article about the lawyer, she turned the paper over. A cloudy photo showed a line of people being served out of a giant stew pot. BENEFIT CHILI SUPPER TO RAISE FUNDS FOR MURDER VICTIM'S MOTHER. Set in the corner was a small, candid shot of the murdered man's mother. She was a thin, older woman whose wispy hair trailed around a haggard face. Karen threw the paper back down angrily.

"What's with you?" Mitch asked.

She glared down at her hands folded on the table. "Everything about this Chelsea case makes me burn. That poor old woman comes back here to get her dead son, and the Chrystals can't even pay her expenses in a lousy fleabag motel — "

"Hey," Pete interrupted. "What makes you think she'd take it if they offered it?"

"She's taking charity from these people."

"Those are Mill people, her own kind," Pete reminded her. "She probably doesn't want anything from the Chrystals except justice."

"She'd do better taking motel money," Karen said. "Fat chance she'll get any justice around here."

"You mustn't have read that paper very well," Mitch said, his tone a little annoyed. "That guy from the state is after Chelsea like a wolf pack, doing everything he can to get her behind bars." He paused, then added quietly, "I wouldn't wish a night in that jail on my worst enemy."

"Hey, hey," Pete intervened. "Make way for burgers and pass the catsup. That kind of talk will turn your stomach."

Not until Mitch rose, saying he had to go back to the shop, did Karen realize how quiet he had been. He hadn't said a dozen words after his remark about the state's attorney.

As he rose, Karen reached up and caught his sleeve, smiling at him. "Hey, you," she said softly.

"Hey, yourself," he said, smiling back and patting her hand. She stared up at him, stunned. Where was the quick kiss dropped on her hair? Or maybe just a rough finger drawn tenderly along her cheek?

But he was gone. She looked after him, feeling strangely hollow.

Chelsea had quit being able to sleep. She would lie in the darkness long after the corridor outside was silent. She watched the moon move slowly past her window with a feeling of exhausted despair. Her new attorney was a hearty, smiling man who did his best to raise her spirits, but nothing he said matched the concern in his eyes. His questions probed and searched, as if he were desperately looking for some hidden fact to help her.

When she finally did fall asleep, it was only to awaken crying from some miserable nightmare. She could never remember these dreams that left her trembling, her gown bathed with sweat.

After a week without rest, she was too tired even to get up and walk around the room. The slightest sound startled her, leaving her heart pounding.

"You *have* to get up and move around, Chelsea," Dr. Gilbert told her. "If you don't, you will be unsteady on your feet when you get out of here."

Chelsea looked up at him. "I don't feel like moving around," she told him, wondering if he really thought she would ever be free to "get out." "The more I think about being locked up behind bars for a murder I didn't commit, the less I care about doing anything."

"You need to build your strength up for your trial," he said. "Lying in bed is weakening." As he spoke, he took her pulse, and made a notation on her chart, frowning to himself.

"Nothing is going to help me," she told him.

He leaned over and took her hand. "Chelsea, dear Chelsea. This whole thing is insane. Nobody believes you killed that man. No jury is going to convict an innocent child. You mustn't ruin your health worrying about it this way."

She tried to keep the self-pity out of her voice and sound like her old, flippant self. "Have you heard of one single thing that contradicts all that evidence they are filling the papers with? There's no hope for me, Dr. Walt. No hope at all!"

He shook his head. "Chelsea, I can't stand your desperate tone. There is hope. You must not let yourself get out of hand like this."

Instead of answering, she began to cry helplessly. He patted her awkwardly, but after a few moments he rang for the nurse, who gave her a shot. As she drifted off, with him still in the chair beside her bed, she caught a few whispered words of his directions to the nurse. "Nerves," she heard. "Vigilance. Depression."

She wanted to protest that her problem was real, not imagined. Instead, the injection made her too dull even to cry out as he left.

After that, she was given an injection every night to make her sleep. But the sleep was not real sleep, only a drugged torpor that she woke from with the same frantic sense of panic she had had the day before. "Please make them let me alone," she begged him. "I just want to be let alone."

"We have to take care of you," he told her gently. "You are too important to all of us. We love you, Chelsea."

She studied him. How could anyone love a girl who was believed to be a murderer? Why should they take care of her when she had no future left at all? It didn't make sense. She wanted to tell him that but knew that if she spoke, those tears would start again, helpless tears she couldn't stop. She wanted to tell him she was nervous because of the tiny drum that seemed to be beating steadily in the back of her head, marking the minutes of the rest of her life. Afraid of crying, she only nodded at him and tried to smile.

He rose with a sigh and touched her shoulder gently. "Any messages for your grandmother?"

Grand Lily. How was she taking this? Grand Lily's heart had given them all some pretty scary times in the past few years. Chelsea didn't dare answer lest Dr. Gilbert hear the fear in her voice. She only shook her head and fought back the tears.

After he was gone, the guards closed the door for regular visiting hours. Only with the doors closed did she feel safe from the prying eyes that sought her out as people walked along the hall.

A sudden dizziness almost overwhelmed her as she sat on the side of the bed. Her jacket had tumbled to the floor. She sighed and made her way across the room to the window, bracing herself from one piece of furniture to another.

Once there, she leaned against the side of the window, trying to stay close to the drapes so that she wouldn't be seen. Her gown, for all that it was a lovely color and feel, clung to her figure like skin, outlining her gently curved figure and the smooth line of her waist and hips. She stared miserably out into the almost full parking lot of the hospital. Cars moved in and out. Couples, arm in arm or carrying packages or flowers, streamed toward the entrance. Neither her mother nor Amy had come that day. Her father, his face gray and drawn, had come and explained that he and Mr. Sexton, her attorney, were making every effort to negotiate a bond with the presiding judge. "It's not been easy," he told her. "The judge is under heavy pressure since the state's attorney got that clean bill of health from the doctor he sent here."

"What does he want from me? Why is he doing all this?"

Her father looked away. "To see a Chrystal in jail, my dear. We are trying equally hard to keep that from happening."

She leaned to pull a single rose from a mixed arrangement, and breathed the wonderful sweetness of it. With the rose still in her hand she turned her head to look at the little pot of African violets still bravely blooming under her lamp. Then, overcome by exhaustion, she dropped the rose on the window ledge and went back to the bed.

Chapter
Nine

Dawn heard the music from Josh's stereo through the rushing water of her shower. Leaving a damp trail on the slate floor, she started for the family room just off the kitchen. The rich aroma of their mother's breakfast coffee still lingered in the air, along with the toasted pecan of Josh's favorite coffee cake warming in the oven.

She wasn't surprised that Josh was still up in his tower room. Except when their mother was around, she and Josh hadn't talked to each other about anything but Chelsea's case since Josh and Pete had their argument. A few times Dawn had really felt bad about the bleak, lonely way Josh moved through the halls at school and moped around at home. He had almost walked Abner's legs off by taking the poor old dog along for company on his own long, late-night walks. But she felt bad about herself, too, worried about Chelsea, unable to say anything to Karen without being jumped on, and it *had* been Josh who caused the rift between her and Pete this time.

She turned the tv on. The screen was coming alive as Josh appeared in the doorway. "Please don't," he said quietly.

She looked over at him. "Please don't what?"

"Turn that thing on," he said.

As she punched the button again, the brilliant screen diminished to a nervous green square of light and then vanished. He had turned toward the kitchen. "I just can't deal with it," he admitted, pulling the coffee cake out of the oven and setting it on a wooden board on the table. "If I could even talk to Chelsea . . . instead I only hear news, bad news getting worse by the day." He turned to her. "They can't put her in jail, Dawn. They just can't do it."

"Her lawyer is fighting it," she reminded him. "They say he's one of the country's best."

The pat of butter on his wedge of coffee cake melted quickly, running in golden streams down the side to gather in puddles on his plate. He only hunched over it, staring vacantly across the table. "Everybody is leaning over backward," he said. "It's all the fault of those milltown people. They are so sure Chelsea is going to get an extra break that nobody dares give her any breaks at all."

She decided to let the crack about milltown pass. He wasn't thinking all that clearly. None of them was. "Eat your breakfast," she suggested, filling his milk glass as well as her own. "Maybe she'll get a break today. Maybe that judge will reconsider and set bond."

With Josh silent beside her, Dawn walked toward the high school steps. She was astonished to see Ian MacFarland obviously waiting at the top of the stairs for them. She frowned. She and Ian had been really good friends when she first came to town. Not only had she liked him but they had a lot in common, because his father and her mother were both doctors in the same hospital. But that had all changed when Ian got a painful crush on her. Even though that was long over, Dawn had sometimes wondered if they would ever get back on a good, friendly basis again. But there he was, coming toward them, his face serious.

"Hey, you two," he said, his voice husky. "I'm dead sorry."

Josh stared at him. "About what?"

Ian made a face and thumped his forehead with the palm of his hand. "That's what I was afraid of. You haven't seen the paper? Read the news?"

Josh's voice came a little high. "What happened? What's wrong?"

To Dawn's astonishment, Ian reached out and touched Josh's arm quickly. His words were almost drowned out by the pealing of the warning bell. "Just take it easy," Ian said. "It's a bummer but there's nothing anybody can do."

Then, with his hand under Dawn's arm, Ian

87

led her inside, leaving Josh staring after them.

"Ian," she cried. "What in the world is going on?"

He kept looking straight ahead. "Dirty, filthy pool," he said, talking faster than he usually did. "Some vicious clown got an indecent picture of Chelsea in her hospital room. No clothes on, or worse. You'll see enough copies around school, you can bet. They published it on the front page of a special edition of the *Mountain Gazette* early this morning."

Dawn stared at him. This was impossible. "But she's under guard," she told him. "No one is allowed in there except —"

"Telescopic lens," he explained. "That's what the police are guessing, anyway. The authorities have already launched an investigation into who took it." Only then did he look down at her, his eyes sober on hers. "I just didn't want you and Josh to run into it cold turkey."

She tightened his arm against her side. "Thanks, Ian," she whispered. "Thanks for trying."

Ian was right about the pictures being everywhere. The hall was clumped with groups of kids tittering and leering at someone's folded newspaper. Dawn, with her head high, passed group after group, refusing even to glance at what they were making such fools of themselves over.

Her luck failed just outside class. Perky Palmer and Ryan Simpson, heads together, saw them coming and held the picture out. "You've seen the shot of the century, haven't you?" Ryan asked. "Now that is a body!"

Dawn felt her face redden with shame and anger, but the picture imprinted itself on her mind anyway. The photo was of poor quality but painfully clear. It didn't look candid at all, but more like a carefully posed ad for a magazine. Chelsea, her head half turned to expose that perfect profile, stood against a flowing drape holding a single rose in her hand. A single bold headline ran above the picture of this glowingly glamorous girl: TOO SICK FOR JAIL OR JUST TOO RICH?

Ian had said, "No clothes or worse." Somehow it was worse. The gown Chelsea was wearing was so sheer and low-cut that it seemed designed to be provocative. Lines of lace barely crossed her breasts toward the shoulder. The fabric clung to Chelsea's waist and hips like a gleaming glove.

In spite of herself, Dawn gasped as Ian steered her past. "Jealous maybe?" Perky called after her. Without looking back Dawn knew how Perky would toss that mane of pale hair and laugh up at Ryan for his applause at her cleverness.

"Easy," Ian whispered. "Just take it easy."

Not until Dawn was settled into her chair and felt the color finally cooling from her cheeks did she realize that Pete Carter, sitting just behind her, had held her chair as she sat down. She turned to look at him but he was staring at the front of the room, avoiding her eyes.

Somehow Dawn made it through that crazy morning. The excitement had not even dwindled by noon. Every chance phrase carried Chelsea's name, and the tone was vulgar and demeaning. Dawn was grateful for Ian's counsel. "Easy, easy," she whispered to herself more than once when someone eyed her, smiling, daring her to defend Chelsea Chrystal now.

Josh was waiting for her at the cafeteria door. "Come eat with me," he ordered. "I'm going to put a fist through somebody's face if I hang out alone."

Ian was late into the room. Dawn saw him fill his tray, glance around, and then come toward them, his step remarkably springy. Before Dawn could even say hello, Ian leaned across the table. "To coin a phrase, it's an ill wind that blows nobody good."

Josh glared at him. "Wait," Ian said. "Wait until I tell you." He glanced around as if to see if he were being overheard. "I talked to Dad at the hospital. They are planning to move Chelsea sometime tonight, when the tv and news people have their guards down."

Josh groaned. "No, no," Ian said quickly, still keeping his voice low and confidential. "They are taking her home, where she will be under house arrest after her bond is posted."

Dawn was startled by the instant tears of relief that welled in her eyes. "Thank God!" she said. "What happened?"

"The ill wind," Ian explained. "Dad understands that Judge Harris got so mad when he saw that picture and read that headline that he took it on himself. That's what I meant by the ill wind. That picture is getting Chelsea safely back home.

Dawn smiled back at Josh's sigh of relief. "Ian, thanks. What a break."

Ian shook his head. "Keep it under your hat, will you? They want to keep the move away from the media hawks, if possible."

The timing of Chelsea's move might be secret, but the judge's decision was all over school within an hour. Dawn, listening to the fresh flow of talk, could hardly hold her tongue. She expected the crowing "I told you so" from people who had predicted that no Chrystal was ever going to see the inside of the jail, but it still didn't go down easy.

Karen Pickett, crosser and more restless than usual, was in the hall as Dawn opened her locker to get her coat. Dawn didn't know the red-haired girl Karen was talking to, only that she was a milltown girl who played on the volleyball team.

"Talk about clever?" the red-haired girl was saying in a laughing tone. "What do you suppose old Chrystal had to pay a photographer to take that sexy shot of his daughter? Typical trick for those people. He must have known the judge would give her house arrest instead of jail after that."

Something snapped in Dawn's mind at the words. That was too much! Knowing the Chrystal family as she did, Dawn was shocked that anyone could misunderstand them so completely. What a nasty mind that girl had. She whirled to answer the girl just as someone passed at a dead run. Dawn's books and coat flew out of her arms and slid along the hall. Pete appeared from nowhere with Mitch at his side. Karen turned and watched Mitch pick up books along with Pete.

"Service is pretty good around here, wouldn't you say?" Karen asked the question of Dawn, but her eyes were on Mitch.

"It beats the conversation by a country mile," Mitch replied. Then, with a nod at Dawn, he turned and walked off down the hall with Pete, leaving Karen and Dawn both staring after them.

Before Dawn caught her breath, Karen turned and walked off angrily down the hall in the opposite direction.

Chelsea had been in that hospital room long enough to sense that something new was in the air. So many people had walked past the door by eight o'clock that the guards shut it against their prying eyes. She tried to find out what was going on from the girl who brought her breakfast tray, but the aide only looked away and said, "I don't know what you're talking about."

The tray had still not been picked up when her father came in. He smiled in that painful way, sat down, and took her hand. "Okay, little princess," he said quietly. "You're going to get a chance to prove what you're made of."

She stared at him, suddenly more terrified than she had been even in the darkest of the nights just past.

He was having trouble finding words. Finally he blew out a thin stream of air, breathed deeply, and plunged in. "Apparently some monster has had a camera with a telescopic lens trained on your window. He got a picture, a very damning picture, of you against the light."

"Against the light?" Chelsea asked. This didn't make sense. How could someone take a picture without her knowing it? What did he mean?

He handed her the newspaper, folded so that the picture filled a fourth of the sheet. She stared at it in horror, then shut her eyes tight. *No.* It couldn't be. Yet even with her eyelids pressed so tightly that a dull red glow came, she could still see her entire body, every curve, there in that hateful, smudged newspaper print.

"But Daddy!" she cried. His arms were around her, holding her against the sobs that shook her. Something as painful and searing as fire seemed to flow all over her flesh. How could she ever face anyone again? "No, no, no," she moaned as he rocked her back and forth.

Finally she could breathe again. He handed her tissues one after another until she had her eyes and nose under control. "I might as well be dead," she told him.

He stroked her back gently. "Be strong," he whispered.

"But Mother?" she asked, remembering her mother's pain and withdrawal when her brother Monty had brought such shame onto the family.

"She loves you," he said gently. "And she understands. She was the one who suggested I come right away. She thought you should hear about this monstrosity from me instead of some stranger. I want to assure you that an investigation has already been launched. Whoever did this will be punished."

If they get the right person, Chelsea told herself. How had so much been stripped away from her so fast? Her freedom, her belief in the operation of justice? And now her own sense of decency. How could she ever feel clean again?

The door to her room remained closed all the rest of that day. Between the end of afternoon visiting hours and the arrival of the dinner tray, Dr. Barbara Newhouse let herself in the door and crossed the room to drop a kiss on Chelsea's forehead.

Chelsea let Dawn's mother take both her

hands and sit quietly a minute. She had always liked Dr. Newhouse, but had never looked at her so clearly before. The late-afternoon sun glistened on Barbara Newhouse's shiny black hair. Her eyes were dark and sensitive like Josh's, but her smile reminded Chelsea of Dawn, open and warm.

"I'm breaking the rules to bring you a message or two," Dr. Newhouse said, grinning. "The nurses out there think I came in to ask you how you're sleeping. Actually I came to tell you that we all love you. I bring you love from both my children. From Dr. MacFarland and Ian." She paused. "I guess you'll never know, Chelsea, how many people are rooting for you."

"But that awful picture!" Chelsea cried.

"That awful picture is somebody else's crime, not yours," Dr. Newhouse replied. After a tap on the door an aide opened it and entered with Chelsea's dinner tray.

After leaning to press her cheek against Chelsea's again, Dr. Newhouse rose. "I leave you to your wonderful meal," she said brightly.

At the door she stopped and turned, looking not much older than Dawn in her trim white smock. "Would you believe that even the boy who fixed my car today asked about you? He said if I saw you, I was to give you a message from him." She grinned. "Not poetic but it was sincere. 'Hang in there!' "

Chelsea stared at her. "Hang in there!"

That had been the message on the card with the violets, and on the crumpled blue note.

"Who was he?"

Dr. Newhouse shrugged and smiled. "Just a nice, curly-headed kid at the auto shop," she said. "I have no idea what his name is."

Chapter Ten

Chelsea walked carefully around her own bedroom. She had the strangest compulsion to touch every object in the room. Not to handle them or move them. She only needed to touch all her things with the tip of a finger to show that they were real and that she was really home. Home, and safe from the prying eyes in the hall, the unknown camera whose telescopic lens had exposed her to the curious eyes of a million strangers.

Amy, in her direct way, challenged Chelsea's despair about the picture. "But the bikini you wear at the club shows twice as much," she told Chelsea.

"That's different," Chelsea snapped at her.

"How is it different?" Amy pressed.

Chelsea studied her sister. "I choose to appear in it," she decided. Then, because that sounded so arrogant, she added, "And all those people are my friends."

"Sure," Amy said. "They're all your friends. So you mean you don't want anyone who isn't our kind to see you undressed?"

"Go away," Chelsea told her. "Just go away, that's all."

She felt rotten. Her head ached all the time, and whenever she stood up, she felt strangely uncertain on her feet. In the hospital she hadn't wanted to get out of bed. Now that she was home, she was too restless even to sit down for more than a minute or two. As happy as she had been to be smuggled out of the hospital by the service entrance and brought home, that drumbeat in the back of her head kept telling her that this was only one step closer to her doom.

"I wish you would try to get some rest," her mother said, eyeing her with concern.

Chelsea shook her head. "It only makes me jumpier to sit down, and I couldn't go to sleep for anything."

"That's just nerves from all this stress, honey," her mother assured her. "Relax and have confidence in your father and Mr. Sexton. The jury selection is going on right now. When this is all over. . . ." Her voice trailed off as she turned away to fool with the flowers that were still coming.

"This room smells like a funeral," Chelsea said.

"What a thing to say. Your friends just care." As she spoke, her mother stopped by the tiny African violet plant. "Did you ever find out who sent this dear little thing? Look at the bloom on it!"

"I never found out," Chelsea said. But she had a clue. The first time she had a chance to talk to anyone, she would find out who the curly-haired boy in the service station was. But that was silly. A lot of people said, "Hang in there." Even when she knew what his name was, it probably wouldn't mean anything.

But then, nothing meant anything anymore. If they convicted her of that murder she would be sent away. If they acquitted her she would have to stay and pretend to be the old Chelsea Chrystal, when down inside she felt filthy and degraded. Chelsea looked up to see her mother watching her, an uncertain, apprehensive look on her face. Having her there was only making the panicky feeling inside worse, but she could hardly ask her mother to go away and leave her alone, as she had Amy.

"I think I need to take a nap," she told her mother.

"What a splendid idea," Mrs. Chrystal said with relief in her voice. She crossed the room quickly and unfolded the satin throw from the foot of the bed to cover Chelsea. Chelsea, watching her mother start for the door in swift, graceful steps, realized that this woman was as relieved as Amy had been to get away from her. Would this be the story of the rest of her life, people looking for excuses to leave her? She couldn't blame them, not really.

Although Chelsea had only suggested the

nap to give her mother a graceful reason to leave, she fell asleep almost at once. When she awakened with a start, it took her a moment to realize where she was. The windowsill in her room was crowded with fresh and different flowers. A brown-wrapped package crowded the African violets on her bedside table.

Hitching herself up on her pillows, she looked at the package. Although it bore no return address, she recognized the immature handwriting on the wrapper, and her heart leaped. This had been addressed by the same person who had sent her the pot of violets and the note in the blue envelope. When she began to loosen the tape on the seams, she saw that the package had been opened before.

Sudden anger throbbed at her temples. What was going on? Who was spying on her, opening her mail? She carried the package to the door and called down the hall to her mother.

"Mom's not here," Amy said, coming out of her room. "She's downstairs somewhere. Can I help?" Then, with a glance at the package, she asked, "What was in it?"

"I don't know," Chelsea told her. "I just wanted to know who had opened it before they brought it to me."

"Probably Zacchary," Amy said. "They've been checking the mail outside since. . . ." Her voice trailed off and she flushed with embarrassment.

"Checking the mail?" Chelsea said. "What's going on here, anyway?"

Amy backed into her doorway. "Maybe you better ask Mom or Dad. 'Scuse me now." As she disappeared inside her room, Chelsea heard the click of her latch.

Chelsea stared at the empty hall a moment and fought those sudden, unpredictable tears. Turning into her room, she tore the wrapper off the box angrily and wadded it up. The box inside was the shape of a shoe box, only a little smaller.

The toy was wrapped in tissue paper. It took Chelsea a minute to figure out what it was. Then, placing the little wooden stand on the table, she realized it was a flat, wooden, carved clown hanging by his hands from the bars of a wire trapeze. He was smiling in that idiotic, painted-clown way. She pulled the string hanging down the side, and he flipped up and over the trapeze two, almost three times before stopping again, right side up, to smile back at her. She grinned and tapped him again before digging through the tissue paper for some sign of who had sent it.

When she finally found the tiny slip of paper, she was not surprised to see the message, written in that same immature hand. "Hang in there. M."

After setting the clown where she could touch it from her bed, Chelsea found an emery board and smoothed her nails. Every time the little clown did his act and came back on his feet smiling, she felt better.

She was smiling when her mother tapped and pushed the door open. "You *did* have a nap," her mother said happily. "And you found your package."

"It had already been opened," Chelsea told her accusingly.

Her mother nodded. "All the mail has to be," she said. "We don't want anything unfortunate to happen."

"Unfortunate?" Chelsea asked. "What is that supposed to mean? Have I had bomb threats or something? Has somebody decided I should be blown away as well as framed for murder?"

"Chelsea, please." Her mother's voice was uneven from stress. "There have been phone calls. Some people don't seem to realize you aren't well. . . ."

"Oh, Mom, I'm sorry," Chelsea said. "Come and look at him. He's just darling!" She tugged the clown's string and watched her mother's face as he clattered his trick.

"He *is* darling," her mother said with relief, sitting on the edge of the bed. "What a thoughtful thing! Who sent it?"

Chelsea impulsively handed her the note. "The same mystery person who sent the violets."

" 'Hang in there,' " her mother read aloud. "What a nice thought."

"The same message came with the violets," Chelsea told her. "And I still haven't figured out who it is."

Her mother smiled and touched her cheek. "Whoever it is, is wonderfully thoughtful," she said. Then, smiling, she pulled the string on the toy herself. "When you solve the mystery, let me thank your shy friend, too."

The jury selection had been going on for three days. Dawn, going through the hall between classes, saw Karen, who was staring at her with a thoughtful frown. Dawn had been wary of Karen since the night of the murder. She didn't have any idea how Karen's foul mood was linked to Chelsea's trouble, but Karen had become so jumpy and edgy and sharp-tongued that Dawn dreaded even having to speak to her. But with Karen practically in her path, Dawn met her gaze. "Something the matter?" she asked.

"Nothing really," Karen said. "I bet you are hoping that they never manage to get that jury together."

"I don't know what I want," Dawn admitted. "I dread the trial, but I want it over, all over."

"It could drag on forever, you know," Karen said. "It isn't going to be easy to find twelve good men and true who believe that a Chrystal should legally get away with murder."

"Karen, that's a miserable thing to say. Chelsea's innocent until she's proven guilty in a court of law."

"You think so?" Karen asked. "Then why are they keeping armed guards around the Chrystal house even after her father posted that enormous bond?"

Dawn looked at her, astonished. "Bill

103

Gurney," she decided aloud. That was it. This had all begun with Mr. Chrystal's fear of the ex-convict Bill Gurney. No matter what had happened up in the woods, he could still be around, waiting for a chance to fulfill his threats.

Karen laughed harshly as she let herself out of the door. "Sure, Dawn. Maybe that's who the bearded man was, Bill Gurney, an old bearded man who turned young and blond to liven up Chelsea's life."

Dawn wanted to scream. "I am fed up," she said to Karen. "I am fed up with all this junk. And mostly I am fed up with you baiting me every time I turn around."

Chapter
Eleven

They were still choosing the jury when the week of Mitch's birthday finally arrived. Pete had finally come up with a smashing idea, and Karen had come up with six more dollars from baby-sitting. She studied the present a long time before she wrapped it. Pete was sure Mitch would love it. The pocket-sized leather case was fitted with a number of small, solid tools that made no sense to her. Even though it came with a dense manual that made no more sense to Karen than the tools did, Pete insisted Mitch wouldn't even need it. He already knew how to use every tool in it.

That only left the problem of Karen getting together with Mitch to celebrate the day. She hadn't seen nearly as much of him as usual in the weeks just past. When she had complained, he only said they had been loading extra work on him down at the garage. It had been a week since they talked about it, and he hadn't once been free to spend an evening with her. She shoved the case aside and curled herself into a ball. She didn't want to complain again about not seeing him. She knew how he felt about being nagged. But not being with him filled her with doubt.

Maybe she loved him too much. Maybe it was dangerous to be so hungry for his company, to want to touch him every time they were together, even at school. Maybe she just imagined he had turned cool and strange, because she wanted to be so warm and familiar. "Nuts," she shouted, scaring the cat off the end of the bed. "I'll just call him and set something up. This is Mitch, you fool, *your* Mitch."

At the garage they said he'd left early. Mitch's mother said she hadn't heard from him. Pete's mother said Pete was out working and she hadn't heard from either him or Mitch.

Karen threw the leather case across the room. It hit the wall and disappeared behind her bed. Let Mitch find her, the stupid lout. She had never chased after a guy in her life and she wasn't about to start now! When her mother came looking for her, Karen pretended to be asleep so her mother wouldn't see the tear stains.

By the time the jury was finally selected, Dawn felt she knew Chelsea's attorney as well as any living man. For all his national fame he was a gentle, thoughtful man when you sat across from him.

"Remember that she's innocent," he told Dawn. "Don't let that attorney rattle you. Just say what you saw and don't let him lead you on. The truth is the only thing that will free your friend."

It was one thing to watch a court scene on tv and another to be a part of it. A hard knot came in Dawn's stomach as Judge Harris took his seat on the bench. Chelsea looked unreal, paler and thinner than Dawn had ever seen her. The jury was the scariest row of people in the whole courtroom. They were all older people, men and women who sat back and stared at Chelsea with hard, flat eyes. Dawn turned around and glanced toward the back of the room for reassurance. Her mother had come and was sitting back there between Josh and her Aunt Vicki. Her mother caught her eye and tightened her mouth in a secret smile that helped until the judge rapped the session to order and the trial actually began.

The state's attorney made the opening statement. He advised the jury that he intended to show that Chelsea Chrystal had provided the dead man, Ralph Schroeder, with money and expensive gifts and then, for reasons that could only be surmised at that point, shot him.

Chelsea's attorney listened to his words intently but raised no objection. When the state's attorney called the defendant, Chelsea Chrystal, to the stand, Mr. Sexton rose and asked that it be made a record for the jury that Miss Chrystal was under no obligation to take the stand since the state had the burden of proof.

"However," Mr. Sexton went on, "since Miss Chrystal has nothing to hide, she has elected to take the stand."

Chelsea answered the state's attorney's questions in a flat, expressionless voice. When he started asking the questions again, jumping around this time, Mr. Sexton rose to object. When the objection was sustained, Mr. Larrimore dismissed Chelsea, but not before he left the jury with the impression that Chelsea was repeating something she had memorized, rather than something that had really happened.

Dawn was the first of the eyewitnesses called. A sudden weakness in her legs made it difficult to walk all the way up to the elevated witness chair. As she repeated the oath, her voice broke a little. Mr. Larrimore glared at her so fiercely that she felt her heart thundering under her dress. He wouldn't let her tell all the story. She could only answer his questions and she could hear her own answers being damaging to Chelsea.

"Did you listen to the defendant's conversation on the telephone?" Mr. Larrimore asked her.

"I didn't listen, but I did hear some of it," Dawn answered.

"What exactly did you hear?"

"She said hello, then dropped her voice."

"To keep you from hearing?"

"She just dropped her voice."

"Did you hear any words aside from hello?"

"She said something about it being dark and there wasn't a road."

"That was all?"

"I think she said, 'Thirty minutes.'"

"What did she say when she came back into the room where you were?"

Dawn felt her hands getting wet. Why did those words sound so ominous? She glanced at Chelsea's attorney, who nodded to her. Dawn repeated the words exactly as she remembered them, exactly as she had repeated them first to the police and then to the grand jury.

"She told me to listen, and said she had to go out for a minute. She told me to wait right there, she would be back."

"You didn't argue with this?"

"I didn't have a chance," Dawn admitted. "She said, 'Just wait. This is something I have to deal with, once and for all.'"

A dreary trail of witnesses followed. The policemen gave their reports in a tedious sing-song and presented diagrams and pictures of the scene of the crime. The stable man, Zacchary, said his piece in a slow drawl that Dawn hadn't noticed before. Amy testified wide-eyed and clear-voiced, followed by her father.

When Dawn next looked back, the seat between Josh and her Aunt Vicki was empty. An awful loneliness settled over her as the parade of witnesses continued.

A teller at the bank testified that shortly after lunch on the day in question, Miss Chelsea Chrystal had cashed in seventeen hundred dollars in government bonds in her name and withdrawn all the cash in her savings account.

The precious-metals dealer testified that he had bought several items of fourteen-carat gold jewelry from Miss Chrystal as well as a quantity of sterling silver.

A forensics expert from the crime lab identified the bullet as having come from the gun found in Chelsea Chrystal's hand, a gun registered to Alexander Chrystal. Again there were diagrams and blown-up pictures of the bullet extracted from Ralph Schroeder's body. He further testified that tests conducted on Chelsea Chrystal's right hand established that she had recently discharged a gun.

Ralph Schroeder's mother stumbled a little on her way to the chair, so that an officer of the court had to brace her arm. A murmur rippled through the courtroom as she took her seat.

The state's attorney's voice turned very gentle.

Had she identified the murder victim as her son?

She had.

Had she known he had come to this area upon being released from state prison?

She had not.

Had she been surprised at his not arriving home?

At that she shook her head. "He had plans to start a gas station up where we live. But first he was gonna earn the money to start. I figured he had gone straight to where this temporary job was and I would hear from him."

The final witness was a maid at the Chrystal home. Dawn nearly died at the woman's testimony. The woman couldn't know what she was saying, how it must sound to the jury.

"She's a butterfly, that girl, as sweet as they come. She's always had more loving and more fun than any living creature. Why, she's so full of fun that there was never a new thing she wouldn't try."

"Would you say she was restless for new thrills?"

Chelsea's attorney objected that the witness was being directed. The state's attorney withdrew the question, but everyone in the jury box had seen the woman's delighted nod at how well he had phrased her thoughts.

Dawn felt weak and quivery by the time the judge recessed the court for the afternoon. She tried to get Chelsea's eyes, but her friend might as well have been turned to stone. With her long, lovely hands folded in her lap, she stared at nothingness, a statue of ice.

"I can't go back to school," Dawn wailed.

"I promised Mom," Josh told her. "Nobody knows how long this will go on."

"Not long, at this rate, I would say," her Aunt Vicki said acidly. "So far they have that poor child dead to rights."

Dawn and Josh had just finished checking in at the office when Karen and Mitch passed with Pete. Karen's face bore that cold, unhappy look that had become habitual with her. Mitch released her arm and came over.

"Did it go as bad as they said?"

"Pretty bad," Josh nodded. "But it's only the first day."

"You mean, the big-gun lawyer hasn't come in to blow justice to bits?" Karen asked acidly.

Something exploded in Dawn's head. "You make me sick, Karen." She didn't even realize she was shouting. "Maybe you'll get your way. Maybe Chelsea will be sent to prison for a murder she didn't do. The only crime Chelsea ever committed was being born rich. If that ex-convict had murdered Chelsea up there in that shack, you would have called him a martyr if he was convicted. YOU MAKE ME SICK!"

Dawn didn't hear the door of the principal's office open behind her. She heard nothing but Karen's screech of fury as she jumped at Dawn, jerking her hair and slapping with her other hand.

Josh and Pete together barely pulled Karen loose. "Liar!" Karen was screaming. "Snob! Liar!"

Then the principal was there, red with anger, his voice cold. "I will see both of you girls in my office immediately."

Dawn's face smarted as she walked inside and took a chair. Outside she saw the principal talking to the boys, all three of them, one at a time. Karen sat down two chairs away, her lovely face livid with rage.

Dawn listened to the principal's lecture with only half a mind. How could she have lost control like that? But she had meant every word she had said. How could she help building up awful resentment against attitudes like Karen's, when Chelsea was suffering so much?

But even as she silently defended herself, she was cringing at what her mother would say. And Aunt Vicki!

The principal's words broke through the fog of Dawn's thoughts. "Very well, Dawn," he said. "In consideration of the stress you have been under these past weeks, especially the strain of testifying today, I will send your mother a written copy of rebuke with a warning. Also, you and your brother will be excused from classes until this trial is completed."

He turned to Karen. "As for you, Karen Pickett, you certainly knew that Dawn would be keyed up after the experience of a day in criminal court. There is no justification for your responding to Dawn's tirade with physical violence. You are under probation for the next six weeks."

When Dawn rose to leave, she tried to avoid looking at Karen. It was impossible to walk by her without seeing her twisted face. Karen's expression said it clearer than words could have. "See what I mean about privilege?"

Pete was waiting outside the office with Josh. Dawn looked up at him, half afraid of

113

what she would see. Then she realized he was holding his arms out to her. She walked into his embrace, near tears to feel the warmth of his strength close around her. Then he leaned so that his whisper was almost lost in her hair. "Hey, Newhouse. How about I come by to see you later? Okay?"

Dawn let Josh lead her outside. The cool air stung her cheek where Karen had slapped her. She touched it with careful fingers. They were at the side of the car when she stopped with a sudden feeling that something had been terribly wrong back there in the hall.

"Where did Mitch go?" she asked Josh.

He leaned over and opened her door from the inside. "I really don't know. When the principal went in there with you and Karen, I watched for a minute. When I looked around again, he was gone."

Chapter
Twelve

Karen stood a moment outside the principal's office. Where was Mitch? What was the matter with Pete and Mitch? Why hadn't they waited for her? She shook her head. She really wasn't operating on all bands. Pete had a class last hour but Mitch didn't. Mitch should still be there, unless he had left for his job without telling her good-bye. But why would he do that?

As for Pete, she had seen him go into that big clinch with Dawn. He never learned, that guy. Just wait, fooling around with a girl like Dawn Newhouse would knock him flat sooner or later.

But that was *his* problem. Her own problem was the cold fear starting in her chest. Why would Mitch go off like that without even waiting for her? None of this made sense.

Karen took the front steps of the school two at a time and raced around the lawn into the parking lot. She heard the motor of Mitch's car before she saw his backup lights turning red as he pulled out.

"Mitch," she called, waving. "Wait up!"

He was halfway backed out when he eased on the brake. His face, indistinct behind the glass, looked strange. Then she saw him duck his head and pull the car back into the parking space. The motor was still running when she reached the door and climbed in.

"Cutting out?" she asked.

With his strong, firm arms resting across the top of the steering wheel, he looked straight ahead and nodded. "You might call it that."

She tried a laugh that didn't work. "Okay, I call it that. Is there something I don't know?"

He breathed deeply, wriggled his shoulders, and then smashed his fist hard against the dash of the car. "Yeah, Karen," he said, obviously fighting to keep his voice under control. "You might say there's something you can't seem to see, and I can't deal with it."

The chill came back, hard and painful in her chest. He hadn't reached out to her. He hadn't even looked at her. For a split second she wished she was back in school, going in late for class. Whatever was coming was scary.

"What are we talking about?" she asked.

"You know I'm better at kidding than serious stuff," he said. "I just know I need to get off and think."

"Is that another way of asking me to get out of your car?" she asked, unable to believe this.

"Not in so many words, maybe, but I'm really mixed up right now. Any way I look at it, things aren't working."

When he turned toward her, the pain on his face tore her up. More than anything she wanted to catch her fingers in his hair and laughingly tug until the two of them were wrestling like puppies. Instead, she was afraid of him . . . afraid even to reach out and touch him.

"Maybe you could think out loud to me," she suggested. Keeping her voice calm was a fight. She felt her fingernails dig into her palms as she clenched her fists.

He looked at her doubtfully a moment before he spoke.

"Karen," he said suddenly, "I can't deal with what's coming down. I keep remembering things too clearly, things you've forgotten. I remember being hauled out of the shop and dragged down to jail with those guys battering me with questions until my brain felt like pulp. I remember them laughing at me, telling me I was going to go to jail when that kid died, telling me I was no better than my brothers and they stunk all the way across the state."

"What's all this?" she asked when he stopped for breath and hit the dashboard with his fist.

"See?" he challenged her. "You don't remember. You don't even think about when I was trapped in that jail and nearly railroaded into prison. You don't remember how you felt about justice and privilege and all that stuff then."

"That's crazy, Mitch. Of course I remember."

"Then maybe you've lost your hearing." His tone was heavy with sarcasm.

The parking lot was busy with kids walking by to their cars. Mitch stirred in his seat, obviously as conscious of their stares as she was.

"Buckle up," he said crossly. "If we have to talk it out now, I'm game, but I don't need a grandstand of interested busybodies watching." He backed the car out with a squeal and burned rubber turning onto the street.

Startled into silence, Karen said nothing as he drove out beyond the country club to where the first ridge of the hills started south of town. Once she realized where he was going she felt better. How many nights had they sat on that hill together, locked in each other's arms, watching the moon float steadily across the sky? It was going to be all right. He was just upset. No problem.

But when he turned to her again, his face was still coldly set. "Since all that stuff about the hit-and-run accident seems to have slipped your mind, let me remind you."

"I remember," she protested.

"I don't think you do," he said roughly. "Remember how they never even tried to find the guy who lifted my car and hit that kid? Why should they? They needed an arrest and were happy to take me because I was a mill-towner. And they would have done it except for your friend Newhouse. She fought and badgered and finally sprung me. That kid, new to town, got me out practically on her own. And why? Because she's not into the kind of back-biting hatred that you were spewing on her today."

"Mitch," she yelled, stung by his tone as much as by his words.

"You wanted me to talk, now listen. Something doesn't ring true about this whole Chelsea Chrystal thing. Her story makes sense to me, okay; why won't anyone else buy it? Timberline is a lonely road. Pennsylvania has its share of bearded men. And I know I'd take a lot of chances to save my family, if somebody was threatening them and Pop was too bull-headed to protect himself. And besides, why should Chelsea try to buy any guy's affection with money and presents? That's stupid. She could have any guy in this town by crooking a finger at him and she darn well knows it."

"Oh, come on, Mitch," Karen scoffed. "You know how Chelsea is!"

"Yeah. I do know how Chelsea is. She's a party girl and she's always up for what's new. But she's not mean and she's not cruel. If you want cruel, go for that Palmer witch or Wimp Simpson."

Karen stared at him, struggling for words. He didn't give her a chance.

"Let me tell you who has her head on straight. It's Newhouse. She's right on the button, Karen. You talk about milltown people being trapped in their positions. How about the Hill kids? They're the flip side of us. They may have a lot of *things*. But when they're in trouble, like Chelsea Chrystal is right now, they have as many or more enemies than we do. Their enemies are different. They're people like you with no power and no money. But the hate you've been spewing on everyone about this just plain turns my stomach."

"Mitch, come on," she pleaded, unable to bear the waves of pain that came with his words.

"Come on, yourself. I feel sorry for Chelsea Chrystal. She's just as trapped as I was. She's out there all alone except for Newhouse. You saw her country club friends giggling and chortling over that nasty picture. It's been building up in me and today it got to be too much. I couldn't deal with that scene you started today. I don't even want to deal with you right now. I'm not sure I want to, ever."

As he talked she had been struggling for breath. She stared at him, knowing the curve of his face with her hands like she knew her own, knowing how his skin smelled close against her, the pressure of his lips.

She needed to argue with him, to set him straight. Instead she could only whisper his name. "Mitch."

"It's no good, Karen," he said, staring through the window that dull way.

She watched him a minute. He was wrong about her. She had just lost her head. His coldness had flipped her out. But he had a memory she could stir.

"Mitch," she repeated, moving toward him across the seat. With one hand on his thigh, she reached up and pulled his head toward hers. His neck was stiff against her but she persisted until his face was close to hers. As she moved her lips onto his, he twisted away to stare straight forward again.

"Are you through?" he asked.

His words were like ice water in her face. She felt herself flush with shame. This wasn't Mitch; it couldn't be! Did he think he could get away with treating her like this? He was crazy, completely crazy. When her breath came back, a flood of words came with it. "Am I through? You bet your life I'm through, Mitchell Boyd. Through for good. Through forever. Through!"

As she spoke she tugged at the door handle and jumped out onto the matted grass beside the road. "Look how lucky you are!" she spat back at him. "This frees you up in case Chelsea Chrystal decides to crook her finger at you. Fat chance, Mitchell Boyd, very fat chance!"

His voice sounded tired, almost bored. "Get in the car. It's a long way back to town."

"I can manage. Believe me, I can manage. What I don't need is more of your deep, deep thoughts."

He looked at her a long moment. "You're welcome to ride back," he offered again. "It'll take you an hour to get down that hill."

"I've got an hour, thank you," she told him.

He frowned thoughtfully. "I don't," he said. "I'm due at the shop right now. But listen to me, Karen. Something's wrong with your head on this. You know how they say that there are lights on but nobody at home? Think about it. Just think about it."

She watched him start the car and turn it around. He stopped and waited again before starting down the hill, leaving her to the gathering dark and silence.

Chapter Thirteen

Dawn felt as if Pete had saved her life. She had come out of the principal's office trembling all over. Just that minute in his arms had been priceless. Then, knowing he would come by after school helped her cope with the ugliness of that scene with Karen.

Karen wasn't like herself anymore. Sure, she had always been quick to take offense and honest to the point of rudeness. This was different. She had been acting like a mechanical toy that had been wound up too tight. It didn't matter. Dawn wasn't going to give her another chance to dump on her.

Dawn was walking Abner in the woods behind the house when she heard Pete drive up. Although she had the dog on the leash, he was tugging her along after him as he bounded around the house to greet Pete. Pete grabbed the dog's paws and danced him in a circle before letting him down.

"Now it's your turn, Newhouse," he said, taking her around the waist. She gasped for air, then clung to him as he swung her dizzily around and around.

"Beg me to stop before we both fall down," he called after a minute.

"I like it," she said, tightening her arms around him.

Abner, excited by their game and unable to keep up with the leash on Dawn's wrist, was circling them madly. Unfortunately, every time he circled, he looped the leash around Pete's legs. One turn proved too many and Pete and Dawn went down together. Abner, delighted at this new game, jumped back and forth over them, lapping at their faces with his tongue.

Dawn heard the tower window open above them. "Hey," Josh yelled down. "Pete's wanted on the phone." After an astonished look at Pete, Dawn grabbed the leash and helped free him. Who in the world would know that Pete Carter was at her house?

"Get the phone just inside the kitchen door," she told Pete. "I'll be right along."

By the time she had Abner fastened and made it indoors, Pete was replacing the receiver.

"Nothing's wrong," Dawn said firmly, not liking the expression on his face.

He shrugged. "I have to make a run into the country for Mitch. That's not the problem." Pulling Dawn toward him with a gentle hand, he held her close, with one hand pressing her head against his shoulder. "The problem," he whispered, "is that I don't want to leave my girl. I've missed you, Newhouse. Nobody knows."

"Nobody knows," she echoed, knowing it wasn't true. She at least knew how hungry she had been for his touch, to be near him like this.

"Hey," he said. "Maybe you could ride along. We wouldn't be more than an hour."

Dawn glanced at the kitchen clock. What a temptation. It was her turn to fix dinner for herself and Josh. But Josh was always delighted to have pizza brought in. It would be easy to pick it up on her way home. She didn't have homework for the next day. Every hour she could keep her mind from the trial was a bonus. Before she got all her good reasons figured out, Pete went on.

"I don't know what's up, but Mitch asked me to drive out toward the hills on the south road and watch for Karen. He says she's walking home from out there."

"Walking home from the hills? Is that all Mitch said?" Dawn asked.

Pete nodded. "I wish I could say I was really surprised, but I'm not. Mitch has really been torn up about this Chelsea Chrystal murder charge. He's convinced she's being railroaded just the same way they tried to railroad him. Everything Karen says puts his teeth on edge."

"Two of us," she told him. "I know how he

feels. I never meant to blow up, but she's really made it tough to keep my mouth shut."

He slid his arm around her. "Come on. I'll put a muzzle on her and make her ride in the backseat."

Dawn laughed. "Maybe I should take a rain check. There's a limit to how dangerously I want to live."

He nodded and pulled her close again. "I can't say that I blame you. I'm not looking forward to this myself. And I'm really sorry we didn't get a chance to talk about Chelsea's trial. Mitch has got me all mixed up, carrying on about it all the time. He's sure there is something missing, something really off-key about the whole thing." He smiled. "He says a good mechanic can hear when something is out of adjustment, and this whole Chelsea thing is wrong."

Dawn nodded. "I'm with Mitch all the way. I was there and I know she didn't do it."

"Does this business about the bearded man bother you?" he asked.

She nodded. "I was mad as anything when Elkins said that about Chelsea not having enough imagination to make up a bearded man, but he's right, Pete. Chelsea isn't long on imagination. That's why she's always grabbing on to something new to amuse her. She can't think things up by herself. That's why the business about the bearded man drives me crazy."

He held her loosely in his arms, frowning.

"Too bad we can't take the top off that silly head of hers and look inside. Maybe there's something in there that she hasn't come up with. Something that would help her get off."

Dawn stared at him, startled. "Pete Carter, am I hearing you say that you want Chelsea to get out of this mess?" That seemed impossible, remembering his bitterness that first day.

He grinned sheepishly. "Big switch, eh? Let's just say that Mitch has worn me down so much that I can even deal with a Chrystal getting away with murder."

She battered his chest with her fists. "Hey, watch that!"

He laughed and held her tight until she stopped her fists. "I love it when you pit your puny strength against my Tarzanlike body," he said, laughing. "The honest truth is that I want what you want, Newhouse. Somehow that's enough for me."

"Right now I have what I want," she whispered. "If things are like they sound, Karen is the one who needs a friend right now."

She could still feel the pressure of his lips on hers as she watched him back up and start down Timberline Drive.

Karen sat down on a flat stone beside the edge of the road where Mitch had left her. An emptiness had replaced her anger. Mitch couldn't be gone, he simply couldn't. She had spent too much of her life loving him. This

127

was a spat, a lover's spat. He was just being a soft touch for Chelsea because of his own rough time in jail.

One of the things she had always loved him for was his soft heart for people in trouble. That was what had twisted his head around about Chelsea. Like Newhouse; big, soft heart and a head to match.

He would be back. Any minute now that little red car would come laboring back up the hill for her. She wiped her face with the back of her hand and wished she had a handful of tissues. She was going to feel like a fool when he came back and found her bawling on a rock like an absolute ninny.

She rose, brushed off her jeans, and started down the road toward town. The dusk was settling on the side of the hill. Animal noises she had never heard from inside his car came from the woods along the road. When an owl hooted, she jumped and began to walk faster, breathing hard from exercise or fear, she wasn't sure which.

She saw the lights of the car coming clear down the winding road. She ran her fingers through her hair and tucked in her shirt. When he came around that bend and caught her in his headlights, she was going to be swinging along merrily, not slouching like something he could throw away on a hillside after all these years.

Because of the gathering darkness and the blinding light from the car, it took her a minute to realize it wasn't Mitch's car at all, but Pete Carter's.

He slowed to a stop and called to her. "Hey, Karen. If I turn around, will you still be going my way?"

"What are you doing up here?" she challenged him.

"I came to get you," he said, getting out on his side of the car to stretch. "Jump in."

"Did Mitch call you?"

"From the shop where he was working."

Karen opened the door and slid in. Then Mitch was sorry. He was sorry but he couldn't leave work, so he had sent Pete. She said nothing until Pete had the car turned around and was following the winding road back toward town.

"What did he say?" she finally asked.

"That you would be walking down the hill in the dark and would I go pick you up."

"Nothing else?"

Pete shook his head.

"He didn't say why I was up here?"

Pete glanced at her. "He only said you refused to come home with him and would I come drive you down to town."

"He didn't tell you why?"

"Hey," Pete protested. "Whatever you two are into is none of my business. Don't give me the third degree."

They rode awhile in silence. At the city limits the traffic got denser. "Want to drop me at Mitch's shop?" she asked him.

She felt his glance rather than saw it. "What's the matter?" she asked. "Don't you think that's a good idea?"

"No, I don't," Pete told her.

"Don't be silly, Pete," she told him. "Would he have sent you to bring me back to town if he was still mad at me?"

She hadn't realized they had reached her own house until he pulled into the curb. "You must be having trouble remembering your own guy," he said. "Sure he would have sent me. There isn't a mean bone in Mitch's body. He wouldn't leave anybody to walk down that hill in the dark if he could prevent it."

The truth of his words stung hard. "Especially not Chelsea Chrystal," she said acidly.

He didn't look at her, but only shook his head. "Boy, you do have a bad case, don't you?"

His tone was a slap that brought her near tears. Jumping out, she slammed the door hard. "Thanks for the charity drive." There was more she wanted to say, but she didn't want Pete to hear the tears in her voice. Holding her back as straight as she could, she walked up the front walk to the porch without looking back.

The note under her picture on the table was in her mother's handwriting.

"Dad and I at benefit for Mrs. Schroeder. Bingo at the church. Come over if you want. Love."

130

The cry didn't help. The leftover meat loaf sandwich with a Coke didn't help. The energy of her hurt finally turned back to anger. She looked for Mitch's birthday present frantically for a half hour, before remembering it had fallen behind her bed. She would show him. She would show both of them.

The man who ran the little import shop where she had bought the tool case for Mitch was getting ready to close up for the night. Seeing her through the glass door, he smiled and let her in. "I hope it's something quick," he told her, letting her in. "I'm already late getting home."

"I just wondered if I could get a refund on this," she said, holding out the leather case.

"Refund?" he asked. "No problem. Those are hard to get and easy to sell."

He examined the set and then opened the cash register. "I remember. Pete Carter was with you when you bought this. He comes in here a lot with a kid he calls Mitch. Now there's a kid who knows tools." He counted out the bills and then the change into her hand. "And toys," he added. "He bought a toy in here for his girl a week or two ago, one of the best-engineered toys I've ever had."

She stared at him. "For his girl?"

He nodded. "Had it wrapped for mailing. I told him I hoped she liked it as well as I did."

She was still standing outside the shop with the money clutched in her hand when he locked the door behind him.

"You all right?" he asked, hesitating.

She nodded at him. "I'm just trying to decide what to do now," she lied to him. Only as he turned the corner and disappeared did she realize it hadn't been a lie at all.

What did she do now? What could she possibly do without Mitch?

Chapter Fourteen

Dawn was startled to hear the door bell ring a little after ten. Abner, roused from a nap by the fire, staggered to his feet and raced across the slate hall to bark and lunge at the door. Dawn glanced toward Josh's tower room, half wishing he were downstairs. That was silly. Who was going to give her a hard time with all eighty pounds of Abner ready to defend her?

Yet she stopped inside the door to call out, "Who's there?"

"It's me, Karen," came muffled through the wood paneling. Dawn swung the door open, startled. Karen had never been to the new house on Timberline Drive. As Karen stood in the flood of the porch light, Dawn was reminded of the first time Karen had ever visited her. They had been living in the apartment then, and Mitch had just been arrested for the hit-and-run accident. That time Karen had been flaming with fury. Now she stood silent, looking smaller than usual, as if the pain that had faded the color from her face had shrunk her solid, athletic body, too.

"I came to apologize," Karen said. "I'm sorry I jumped you today."

"Come on in," Dawn said, at a loss for words.

Karen shook her head. "I can't.. I just came to say I hope it gets straightened out about Chelsea." As she spoke, Dawn realized that the car idling in the road beyond was a taxi. She could see the light on the front of the car roof. Karen taking a cab clear up Timberline Drive for an apology?

What could Dawn say? One thing about Karen's fine, direct eyes, it was silly to try to lie to her. "It doesn't look good for Chelsea so far," she told her. "Maybe there'll be a miracle."

"You really think she's innocent, don't you?" Karen asked.

"I really do," Dawn admitted. "I was there and saw the gun fall out of her hand, but it still doesn't ring true."

Karen, still unmoving, caught her upper lip between her teeth. "Then what's going on? Is she hiding something to protect somebody?"

Dawn shook her head. "I'm sure she thinks she's telling all she knows."

"Maybe hitting her head gave her amnesia like you had after your accident," Karen said thoughtfully. Then, shifting her weight from one foot to the other, she thrust her hand out.

134

"None of my business, anyway. But I'm sorry about today, okay?"

Dawn caught Karen's hand and held it tight a minute. "Okay, Karen."

Dawn knew Karen's walk well. It was a great walk, springy and vital like an athlete's, yet wonderfully feminine because of Karen's shapely body and legs. The girl walking down the path could have been a stranger. All the life was gone from her step as it had been from her face.

Dawn wanted to run after her, to hold her. She knew too well how it felt to have the boy you loved reject you. But she wouldn't dare try that with Karen, whose pride was as stiff as her spine. Then the taxi door slammed and the lights moved off down Timberline Drive toward town.

Dawn almost couldn't stand to look at Chelsea that morning in court. Winter sunlight streamed through high windows, lighting Chelsea's pale hair and setting a glow on her perfect face. It glinted on the gold heart locket gleaming against Chelsea's white angora sweater. But she didn't look like a real person at all. Her skin looked waxen and the hands in her lap were as still as if they had been carved for a statue.

Bradley J. Larrimore rose briskly to complete the presentation of the state's evidence against Chelsea Chrystal. His air of arrogant confidence made Dawn furious. It also made her a little angry at Mr. Sexton. Through the long parade of witnesses and experts, Mr. Sexton had sat quietly, seldom cross-examining witnesses or challenging Larrimore's procedure. It was as if he didn't care, as if he, like Chelsea herself, had given up. Only when Larrimore smiled at the jury winningly and stated that the state rested its case did Chelsea's attorney rise to request an audience with the judge.

The crowd stirred restlessly during this recess. Dawn heard someone whisper behind her that Sexton would be trying to get the judge to dismiss the case on inadequate evidence. His companion snorted, "Fat chance of that! They've nailed that little Chrystal girl down."

"I hate this town," Dawn told herself miserably. "I hate this town and everybody in it." She closed her eyes hard to hold back tears. When she opened them, the judge and Mr. Sexton were returning. Almost at once, Mr. Sexton opened his case for the defense.

That day seemed to last forever. It took Dawn a while to figure out what Mr. Sexton was trying to do. Chelsea again took the stand and repeated her story in detail.

The state's attorney, Mr. Larrimore, was disgusting. He sat and stared off into space with an amused smile on his face during all her testimony. To look at him you would have thought the whole defense was a useless drill. Mr. Sexton's extended questions about the bearded man brought bored stares from the jury. Someone yawned when Chelsea tried to explain her father's feeling about paying an extortionist and her own terror that the man would injure her family.

A hush did fall on the courtroom when her attorney asked when she had first seen Ralph Schroeder. She glanced up at him and frowned, as if her mind had come from a long way away. "I never saw him," she told him.

"You mean you never saw him alive?" he asked.

She shook her head. "I never saw him at all. As I told you, I started in the door, something knocked me against the wall, and the gun exploded, hurting my hand. The next thing I remember is being in the hospital and hurting all over."

Ralph Schroeder's mother, who had sat through the entire proceedings in a seat just behind the state's attorney, stared at Chelsea steadily.

"And when did you first see the gun?"

"I never saw it, until they showed it here in court," she told him. "I only felt something explode in my hand just as I blacked out."

"Have you ever fired a gun?" he asked.

The state's attorney rose to object, but Chelsea's answer came too quickly for him. She glanced at her father and said, "Oh, goodness, no. Daddy would never hear of it." A soft ripple of laughter stirred the room. Dawn thought she saw Mrs. Schroeder smile.

Sexton then called a series of witnesses who made small cracks in the state's case through expert testimony.

A forensics specialist testified that indeed, if a gun was held in the defendant's hand and fired, it would be impossible to tell whether she or the person holding her hand had actually pulled the trigger. A physician called as an expert witness testified that it was fairly common for the victim of a concussion to have poor or no memory of events occurring at the time of the injury.

It was late in the afternoon, very near the hour for recess, when Dawn saw Chelsea turn very pale. She glanced around at her mother just as Chelsea, with a little moan, slid from her chair onto the floor.

Chelsea felt the members of the jury studying her face. She felt Josh's eyes, too, clear from the back of the room, Josh's eyes and Dawn's and Dr. Newhouse's. What were they thinking? It didn't matter. She had only realized how changed she was when she saw Josh. Always before, just seeing him brought a secret smile and a little leap of joy inside her chest. That had left, along with all her other feelings. The only way to explain why her heart didn't leap at the sight of Josh and why she couldn't feel warmed by Dawn's expressive eyes on her face was that she was dead.

The Chelsea Chrystal this court was trying was someone else, someone she didn't know, someone who made up stories about bearded men, and threatening phone calls, and then shot strangers in a dark cabin. Maybe living and breathing did go on after the real you had been destroyed. She held her body carefully still to conceal the icy shudder that ran along her back. It didn't work. She felt herself swaying, and clutched at the arm of her chair, trying to fight off a sudden black dizziness. People were crying out, and she heard the scrape of chairs as her grip on the chair arm failed, and she felt herself falling.

Chelsea opened her eyes slowly, hearing her heart beating too loudly under her sweater. Dr. Barbara Newhouse's face was very near, smiling.

"There you are, Chelsea," she said softly. "Don't move. Give yourself a minute."

"What happened?" Chelsea asked. "What's wrong?" The walls of the room were covered with bookcases. Slanted light from a louvered window fell across a polished desk.

"You fainted," Dr. Newhouse explained. "One of the more dramatic side effects of the kind of sustained stress you have been through."

"I'm sorry," Chelsea told her. "I have really tried to do it right."

"I know you have. Everyone understands. How are you now?"

"This is Judge Harris' chamber," Chelsea said as she was helped to her feet. "I'm really sorry."

"Can you go back now?" Barbara Newhouse

asked. "Your attorney thinks it's very important."

Chelsea nodded, then added, "Nothing is going to help, you know."

"I don't know that at all," Dr. Newhouse said, reaching for the door handle. "Oh, I almost forgot. I saw the young man with the curly hair again at the body shop. He sent you the same message about hanging in there. This time I remembered to get his name."

Chelsea clung to Dr. Newhouse as they passed through the door. "Mitchell," Dr. Newhouse was saying quietly. "His name is Mitchell Boyd."

Chelsea stared at her. Mitchell. M.

Back in her seat, she let her eyes move over the faces in the courtroom. He was in the back row, his broad shoulders solid and substantial against the pale wall. A loose curl had fallen over his forehead and his eyes were intense and unsmiling. Only when he saw her eyes on his did he come alive. A half smile changed his face and she saw him raise his right hand, only to the shoulder, in a gesture that assured her that everything would be all right.

Something wonderful exploded in her chest. She hardly knew him. After all, he was Karen Pickett's guy. But he was a milltown kid. According to the rules, he ought to hate her and want her dead. But he didn't. He believed in her when he didn't have to. She straightened in her chair. She wasn't going to listen to what went on in the courtroom the rest of the time. She would only think about

Mitch's secret messages, crumpled pieces of blue paper, that funny clown that went over and over the trapeze but always hung on. Most of all she thought of the pale blue violets that had kept on blooming steadily, like a promise.

After her mother brought Chelsea back from the judge's chambers, Dawn stared at her friend in disbelief. Chelsea seemed to be the only person in the courtroom who didn't realize how badly her defense was going.

When Mr. Sexton rose to request an early adjournment due to the lateness of the hour and the indisposition of the defendant, Judge Harris agreed.

When Dawn walked out of the hall of justice, she saw Pete leaning against the railing, talking to Mitch. Excusing herself from her mother, she joined them. Pete, unsmiling, barely greeted her. "Did it go as badly as Mitch said?" he asked.

"Whatever he said, it did," she said. "She passed out. I guess Mitch told you. She passed out and they made her come back in there, and all the time that other attorney was sitting over there laughing."

"Laughing?" Pete said.

"Well, smiling in a superior, nasty way. I don't know why they can't see that she's telling the truth. They keep asking her things she doesn't remember."

"Like?" Pete asked.

"Like when she first saw the dead man and when she first saw the gun and did she ever fire a gun?"

"And she doesn't remember any of that?" Pete asked.

"You can't believe how dark it was, pouring rain and thunder and no light in that cabin at all. I keep thinking about what you said, Pete, that somebody should lift the top off Chelsea's head and see what's in there that she's not remembering. And Karen asked if maybe the concussion had given her amnesia. I don't know what to think."

At the sudden silence between the two boys, Dawn looked up at them. "Now what?"

"Your mother's a doctor, isn't she?" Pete asked.

"You know she is," Dawn snapped.

"Don't they use hypnotism over at the hospital for smoking cures and some minor surgery? Didn't I hear that?"

Now both Mitch and Dawn were staring at Pete. He shrugged. "So what's the difference between looking into someone's head and hypnotizing her to see what else she remembers?"

"Wait," Dawn said. "Wait right here." She looked around frantically. Josh and her mother were both in the car, waiting for her. "Come on, you two. Let's give it a try."

"You go," Mitch said. "I've got to book on to my job. But call me if anything happens," he added. "Anything at all."

Chapter Fifteen

Dawn opened the back door of her mother's car and slid in, making room for Pete beside her. "Mom," she began quickly, "Pete and I have something to talk to you about."

With Josh and her mother twisted in their seats to listen, Dawn made the best case she could for having Chelsea hypnotized. Josh frowned silently but Barbara Newhouse shook her head. "No," she said. "Absolutely no. Dawn, that's really a wild idea, completely crazy. Surely Chelsea knows what she saw. And she's repeated it a dozen times with scarcely a word changed. It has to be all she remembers."

"Remembers!" Dawn repeated, her voice turning insistent. "There has to be more than she remembers. She didn't see enough. You heard her. She doesn't even remember seeing the wounded man. If she shot him, she had to see him to aim at him. She would have seen him, anyway, if her head had been working. I saw him plainly enough and Chelsea was still there when I was, trying to drag herself to her feet and staring that funny way she did."

"But look at the complexity of it," Dawn's mother protested. "Chelsea herself might not want to be hypnotized. Also, she's a minor, which would make it necessary to get her father's permission. Then, of course, her lawyer would have to be consulted. Judge Harris is going to open those proceedings at nine tomorrow morning. We could go through all of that and it could still not help at all in the end."

Josh stared silently over the wheel while they argued. The parking lot had almost emptied. Dawn didn't see the freckle-faced newsboy coming toward the car until he thrust a paper in the window at Dawn's mother. "Paper, lady?" he asked. "The betters are making ten-to-one odds that Chrystal will get it for first-degree murder."

Barbara Newhouse gasped and shoved the paper away. Pete, sitting behind her, called the boy back as he started away. Handing him a coin, Pete pulled the paper in the back window.

For a moment there was no sound in the car but the rustle of the paper. "Okay," Dawn's mother said in a resigned tone. "Let me see what it says."

"You don't want to see it," Pete told her. "Along with the odds on Chelsea's conviction, they ran that sexy picture again."

She turned to stare at him. "They didn't."

144

"They did," he replied, his tone flat. As serious as the situation was, Dawn swallowed a giggle as her mother's dark eyes locked with Pete's.

Reaching back, Barbara Newhouse took the paper from Pete, studied the front page a moment, then turned to Josh. "I need to make a run by the hospital."

Dawn felt Pete's hand grope for hers. The wonderful warmth of his touch was only partly spoiled by the pain of his grip.

"Okay if Dawn rides with me?" Pete asked. "We could meet you over there."

She nodded, then added quickly, "I'm not promising anybody anything."

Dawn was surprised at how quickly her mother reappeared at the hospital door. Instead of joining Josh, she walked straight to Pete's side of his car and leaned to him. "Thank goodness you waited," she told Pete. "I'm willing to be helpful but this isn't my project."

"What does that mean?" Dawn asked.

Her mother straightened so that Dawn couldn't see her face. "I called Chelsea's attorney from inside. He's expecting us at his rooms in the Chrystal Falls Inn."

"Surely not me, too," Pete said.

"You'd better believe it, Pete Carter," Barbara Newhouse came back quickly. "There's an old Chinese saying that he who hatches egg raises chick."

"That's Chinese?" Pete asked, grinning.

"Loose translation," she told him. "Josh and I will meet you in the lobby."

Pete groaned as he started the motor. "Can you tell me how I got into this?"

Dawn, watching his face in profile, stifled a giggle and looped both her arms around his neck. She missed his mouth with hers. He corrected that quickly enough. When they finally pulled apart, he grinned wickedly at her. "I may need a lot of those reminders before this business is over."

"Fortunately I have an unlimited supply," Dawn told him, snuggling back in her seat.

Alexander Chrystal had "spared no horses" as Pete put it. He had housed Jerome Sexton in the VIP suite of the Chrystal Falls Inn. A young man Dawn had never seen before let them in and then disappeared off into another room. Mr. Sexton had replaced his suit coat with a shiny, dark-green jacket with satin lapels and a tie belt with tassels. He had obviously been working when Dr. Newhouse called. Two briefcases stood open beside a coffee table covered with papers and yellow pads.

After nodding at the others, he took Dawn's hand. "I have a weakness for loyal friends," he said. "Come sit here by me and let's hear what is important enough to delay my evening meal."

When he looked expectantly at Barbara Newhouse, she shook her head. "I was dragged into this. Let the kids tell you. It's their idea."

Dawn swallowed hard and tried to begin at the beginning. "One of my friends suggested that if we could take the top of Chelsea's head off and see what she's not telling, maybe the trial would go better." At Mr. Sexton's amused twinkle, she hesitated.

"No, go on," he urged. "That was just such an intriguing picture. So?"

Pete spoke up. "We figured the closest thing to that would be to hypnotize her," he said. "We wondered. . . ."

Mr. Sexton studied Pete. "An interesting idea. Explain what you hope to gain through hypnosis."

"It doesn't make any sense that she can't remember seeing that man, that she can't remember firing the gun," Dawn said. "Mostly she talks about the pain, hitting that door, and her hand hurting and blacking out. See, I had amnesia once and I wondered if the concussion might have buried stuff she saw."

"What do you think about this theory of theirs, Dr. Newhouse?" he asked.

She shrugged. "I thought it was insane when I first heard it, but it has grown on me. For one thing, it's the only new idea around right now." She smiled a little ruefully. "We doctors try everything we've ever heard of before giving up on a patient."

"There's a problem of getting a reliable person," he said absently.

"I checked before we came," Dr. Newhouse

told him. "I have a licensed medical hypnotist standing by for our call. In case you want her, of course."

He chuckled and leaned to the left. "Jenkins," he called. The young man who had let them in appeared in the doorway. After introducing Mr. Jenkins as his assistant, he sent the man back into the other room. "Please get Alexander Chrystal on the phone. Tell him I'd like to speak to him privately."

He leaned forward, pressing large, perfectly manicured hands together. His eyes sparkled as he smiled over at Barbara Newhouse. "We lawyers don't dig any graves until we have bodies to fill them, either, Dr. Newhouse. Is this hypnotist of yours discreet?"

"Perfectly," she nodded.

"There's still no guarantee," he told Dawn and Pete. "In fact, we will have cleared only the first hurdle with Alexander Chrystal. He can agree to the plan, but his daughter can either refuse to try or be a poor hypnotic subject. Even if we get wonderful testimony, by law the judge can't permit the transcript of the questioning to be admitted as court evidence."

Dawn felt her heart drop at this. Why had she presumed the judge would admit anything that would make the case clearer? Her dismay must have shown in her face because Mr. Sexton raised his palm to her. "Wait, Miss Dawn," he cautioned her. "If new evidence should surface, we need not tell what led us to it, right?"

Dawn nodded. When Jenkins appeared silently in the doorway, Mr. Sexton rose and left the room.

Pete whistled softly. "This place looks like the setting for a tv sitcom."

"The difference is that all this furniture is real," Barbara Newhouse told him.

When Mr. Sexton returned, he was wearing a casual corduroy jacket, riding pants, and boots. "I took the liberty of changing while I was out," he explained. "In case anyone asks what we were doing tonight, we were invited to see the Chrystal stables. It seemed judicious to dress for the occasion."

This little act only made sense when Mr. Sexton stepped out the front door of the inn. Flashbulbs exploded and a score of shouting reporters had to be pressed back by Jenkins and the doorman to permit Mr. Sexton to get across the walk.

"No comment," Sexton called to them brightly. "Have a good social evening. I intend to." With a wave of his hand, he and Jenkins disappeared into the backseat of the limousine, whose black-tinted glass completely hid them from view.

The moment they were in Pete's car, Dawn turned to him. "What was all that whispered conversation in the hall between you and Mr. Sexton?"

Pete laughed. "He's a canny old walrus," he told her. "Just wait and see."

"Come on," she pleaded.

149

"Come on, yourself." He grinned, driving toward the river and turning left on a deserted street. "So I get to play games with your hot-shot lawyer. It's a small enough prize to get for being sneered at by the help at the inn."

The game didn't last long. Within minutes, the limo from the inn, looking empty behind its darkened glass, glided down the street to pull up alongside Pete's car. Mr. Sexton and Jenkins were instantly out and into Pete's backseat as the limo cruised on. Only when a half dozen cars, one with a radio station's call letters on the side, had passed, following it, did Mr. Sexton and Mr. Jenkins sit up in the backseat and signal Pete to go on. "The media can be oppressive," Mr. Sexton told Dawn with a wink.

They had barely parked along the curve of the Chrystal drive before Josh and Dawn's mother arrived. The hypnotist, a lean woman in her thirties with a puckish smile, stared up at the columns of the Chrystal house and whistled softly. Mr. Sexton, who clearly missed nothing, chuckled as Barbara Newhouse introduced them.

Alexander Chrystal, haggard from the ordeal of the past weeks, welcomed them at the door. "You will understand that I have asked the staff to serve the family in their rooms tonight." Dawn nodded but she didn't really understand until her mother, the hypnotist, Mr. Sexton, and Mr. Jenkins disappeared up the curving stairs to the second floor.

Alexander Chrystal was as gracious as he was nervous during the hour that followed. Dawn was sure it was the longest hour in her life so far. Dawn had hoped to see Chelsea and knew Josh was hoping for the same thing. Instead, the four who had gone up the stairs trooped back downstairs, their faces unreadable.

"Now, if you will join us, young lady?" Mr. Sexton said, taking Dawn's arm.

Floor-length, deep red draperies covered the windows in Alexander Chrystal's study, and the lamplight gleamed on dark, polished wood. With the doors carefully closed, Mr. Jenkins removed a flat tape recorder from his briefcase and set it on the table.

Turning to Dawn, Mr. Sexton became almost stern. "Listen all the way through before you comment. If something strikes you, look up at Jenkins and he will mark it for later reference. When the taping of the session is quite over, you may hear it again and comment if you wish."

Mr. Jenkins listened intently with earphones for quite a few minutes before removing them and turning up the volume so Dawn could hear.

Chelsea's voice was dreamy as if she were fighting sleep. She spoke very slowly, pausing a long time between words except when she became overcome with emotion. Then she merely stopped and had to be prodded to

151

speak again by the hypnotist's questions.

The story of her encounter with the bearded man on the road was exactly as Dawn had heard Chelsea tell it in court. The fear in her friend's hesitant voice made the hair stand up along Dawn's arms.

Chelsea's voice got weaker and weaker as she described tying the pony and approaching the cabin.

"I was crying," she said. "I didn't mean to, but I was so afraid. I didn't have all the money he had asked for and my legs were funny and weak from being scared. When I got to the door, I was too chicken to go inside. The door was standing open and the only noise from inside was the sound of the rain hitting the roof. Something rustled in the woods really close, but I was afraid to look around. I guess I thought it was some wild animal and I didn't want to see what it was.

"And it smelled bad in there, an ugly, musty smell. I knew nobody was there because it was too quiet. Even the birds that always fret with rain in the woods were quiet.

"I couldn't make myself go in, so I called out hello. A dog barked way off and lightning flickered. I panicked. Nothing looked right or felt right. I was turning to run when the door slammed against me. Something dark slapped against the wall above me on the right. My side hurt where the door had hit me and something caught me across the head and smashed my skull on that wall. My whole body hurt, but I knew I mustn't let myself fall down there. I was trying to brace myself on the wall when my hand was suddenly crushed and that awful noise came. A light shot by my leg and disappeared into the floor. I tried to scream but I couldn't make a sound at all. Then it was black, all black."

Dawn looked up to see Mr. Sexton watching her. "Four times," he said. "You looked up at Jenkins four times. Do you remember them?"

Dawn nodded. "I think so. I don't remember her telling about the animal in the bushes before." She hesitated. "The part about the door bothers me. In court it sounded like the door hit and banged her head against the wall. She's talking about something different here." She looked up. Mr. Sexton was nodding for her to go on.

"I don't remember that dark thing hitting the wall above her before. And how could a flash of light going into the floor by her leg kill the man across the room?"

"Would you like to hear it again?"

Dawn shook her head. "Not unless I need to."

He rose and patted her shoulder. "You are priceless, Miss Dawn. Now, if you will wait here for a moment or two, I need to speak to your mother."

Waiting there in that elegant room, Dawn felt a chill of apprehension. She didn't know what she was waiting for. She only knew she wanted to be out there with the others, with Pete and Josh and her mother. Whatever she was waiting for filled her with apprehension.

153

Chapter Sixteen

Dawn had just finished dressing the next morning when she heard the phone ring out in the kitchen. Josh got there first. After nodding and saying a few words, he hung up and turned to her with a strange look on his face. "Mr. Sexton is coming by to pick you up by limo," he said.

Dawn looked at him, startled. "What's that about?"

Josh flipped on the tv. "He suggested we turn on a local news channel."

Naturally an ad came first with a tanned model surfboarding against a backdrop of palm trees. The face of a local reporter, contorted with excitement, followed.

"Protesters began to assemble at the Chrystal Falls Justice Building a little after dawn this morning," he began. The white walls of the building gleamed in the winter sunlight above masses of people behind a police cordon. Even jumbled together and being forced back by the police, Dawn could read the lettering on some of the signs.

QUIT STALLING, SHE KILLED HIM!
MURDER IS ILLEGAL IN USA!
A LIFE FOR A LIFE!

Dawn groaned. "All that hatred! It scares me to death."

"Maybe Sexton will pull it out some way," he said hopefully. "He was up to something last night the way he sent us off home in such a rush."

"What could he do in a single night?" she asked.

One of the things Sexton had clearly not done was sleep. Dark circles hung beneath his eyes, which were streaked with fine red lines. But he smiled like a man with a secret as Dawn climbed into the limo beside him.

"Big day, Miss Dawn," he said. "You have my permission to cross your fingers."

"It was nice of you to pick me up," she told him.

He smiled genially. "It was nice of you and your tall, skinny friend to give me an idea that could break my stalemate."

"Did it?" she asked.

"The game is never over until the last card is played," he told her.

When the courtroom fell silent under the

judge's gavel, Mr. Sexton rose and went forward.

"Your honor," he said. "Ladies and gentlemen of the jury, citizens." He nodded at the packed courtroom. "In view of new information that has come to our attention, I would like to recall certain witnesses for further questioning."

At his words a buzz of curious comment stirred along the benches.

When the state's attorney rose to protest, both attorneys approached the bench for a whispered conference with Judge Harris. Dawn knew Mr. Sexton had won by the way Mr. Larrimore was scowling as they returned.

Dawn watched in fascination as Sexton called witnesses to the stand in an order that seemed to make no sense at first. The first called was Zacchary, the stable man and guard at the Chrystals. Mr. Sexton, after first entering a copy of the photograph as evidence, showed Zacchary a picture of a heavyset, dark-eyed man.

"Have you ever seen this man on or about the Chrystal property?"

Zacchary nodded. He explained that the man, identifying himself as Jake Harrow, had delivered a load of mended harnesses to the stable the Sunday before the murder. Upon seeing the Chrystal brand on the harnesses, Zacchary let him pull his truck into the barn and unload them.

"And the barn is adjacent to and opens into

the garage where Chelsea Chrystal's car is stored?"

At Zacchary's agreement, he was dismissed.

Larrimore's objection that the testimony was irrelevant was denied.

Chelsea, pale and waxen, was then called to the stand and asked if she recognized the man in the photo. After frowning at it a moment she shook her head and said, "No." Setting the picture aside, he displayed a panel of four bearded men's faces, asking if she recognized any among them. She cried out and covered her face with her hands for a moment. When she pulled her hands away, she was crying and her hands trembled.

"Yes," she cried, pointing to the third picture in the group. "That's him. He's the one from Timberline Drive." Then, unable to stop crying, she was led from the courtroom by a matron. The crowd in the courtroom reacted so noisily that the judge had to bang his gavel repeatedly and threaten to clear the room before they were silenced.

In rapid order Sexton introduced three expert witnesses. When the first began to testify the room fell silent, and Dawn saw the jury members leaning to the testimony with rapt attention.

The first man, a ballistics expert, testified that the bullet he was presenting to the court as evidence had been dug from the earth under the door of the hunter's cabin. It matched the bullet that killed Ralph Schroeder and had been established as having been fired from the murder gun.

The next witness displayed blown-up transparencies of a handprint obtained from the doorway to the right of and above where Chelsea's head struck the wall in the hunter's cabin. The attorney said he would ask him to return to identify those fingerprints. The judge had to pound his gavel for order again.

Ralph Schroeder's mother was next on the stand. Sexton treated her gently, asking her to tell him again why she thought her son had not come home immediately after his release from prison.

"He wanted to go straight," she told him. "He was gonna buy a gas station in our town. But he had to do a job first to get the money."

"Do you know what kind of job it was?" Sexton asked.

She shook her head. "Only that it was fast and he was doing it for Bill."

"Do you know the man named Bill he was referring to?"

The question confused her for a moment. "I don't *know* him," she told the attorney. "But I heard a lot about him. Him and Ralph was good friends in prison. He was an older man and had been there a long time. His name is Gurney, Bill Gurney."

Judge Harris was furious at the explosion of sound in his courtroom. He became threatening before the crowd was finally brought under control.

"Do you have any physical evidence that links Bill Gurney to your dead son, Ralph Schroeder?" Sexton asked, as she looked around, confused by the crowd's excitement.

"Oh, yes, sir," she told him. "I kept all Ralph's letters. He wrote a lot about Bill. The last few letters is all full of his plans for this job."

Dawn lost track of how many times the judge refused the state's attorney's objections, as the fingerprint expert identified the prints as those of Bill Gurney.

The final witness was a police artist who testified that he had painted beards according to Chelsea's description on the faces of four photos. The picture she had selected from the group was a photo of Bill Gurney.

"Ladies and gentlemen of the jury, I propose that the introduction of this new element suggests a rethinking of this entire charge against Chelsea Chrystal.

"We know the following about Bill Gurney. He worked in the Chrystal mill where the murder gun had once been kept. He had made public threats to 'get even' with Chelsea Chrystal's father. His handprint was found on the door sill above the point where Chelsea Chrystal's head struck the upright of the door.

"We also have testimony from the stable man at the Chrystal's that this same Bill Gurney was alone in the stable by Chelsea's car the night the clothing she had prepared for him was taken, the same clothing that was found on and with the body of Ralph Schroeder.

"Miss Chrystal has identified Bill Gurney, disguised in a beard, as the man who accosted her on the road.

"Since the young lady has repeatedly insisted under oath that she never saw the victim of the shooting or the gun itself, let us suppose for a moment that she is speaking the truth as she saw it.

"Let us suppose, based on the finding of that second bullet just inside the door, that when the accused entered that cabin, Ralph Schroeder was already dying from a bullet wound previously inflicted. Let us suppose that instead of being hit by a wind-driven door as she thought, she was actually attacked. Say that she was seized at the doorway, had her head slammed against the wall forcefully enough to cause a severe concussion, and had a gun forced into her hand, and that gun was fired in her hand by a stronger hand gripping hers. And I add, ladies and gentlemen, that the severe bruises on her right hand treated in the local hospital support that theory.

"The finding of Bill Gurney's fingerprints above her head where he would have braced himself for that forced shot make it conceivable that Chelsea Chrystal and Ralph Schroeder were both pawns in a deadly revenge plot planned and carried out by Bill Gurney."

Mrs. Schroeder had begun to weep. Aside

from her slow, racking sobs, the courtroom was silent.

Sexton turned and requested an audience with the judge. This worked like a signal on the crowd. Voices rose and reporters clattered as they raced for the back door of the courtroom.

Sexton was in hushed conference at the judge's bench only a moment before the gavel sounded.

Judge Harris spoke slowly into a sudden silence.

"The law demands that a criminal charge must be established by evidence of guilt beyond a reasonable doubt, with the burden of proof resting on the state. The motion for dismissal of this charge against Chelsea Chrystal by her attorney is sustained. The court will issue a warrant for the detention of William Gurney for questioning in the death of Ralph Schroeder. This court is now adjourned."

Everyone was on his feet and talking. Alexander Chrystal, supporting his wife, moved through the crowd toward Mr. Sexton. Dawn, stunned by how fast this long, painful ordeal had come to a close, sat frozen in her seat, staring at him. Then he turned, smiled at her, and winked broadly. She was crying with joy and relief as Pete reached her side.

"What a fox," he said. "What a canny old fox!"

Chelsea, sitting with her head back and her eyes covered by a cold cloth, heard the noise burst from the courtroom and flow through the halls outside. She sat up in fear and astonishment. "What's happening?" she asked the police matron who had brought her there.

The woman smiled. "I'd say something was out of control. Want to try to walk now?"

Chelsea shuddered. The cold terror that had come at the picture of the bearded man simply wouldn't go away. "If you will stay with me," she said. The woman smiled and took her arm.

At the opening of the door, the hall exploded with the photographer's flashbulbs. People were shouting and calling to her, waving microphones over each other's heads. She shook her head distractedly at the confusion. Then she saw her parents, working their way through the crowd. Her mother reached for her, tears streaming. "It's all right, Chelsea," her father called to her. "You're free. You're cleared."

Beyond them in the crush of pressing people she saw her friends. First Dawn and Josh, then Pete, then Mitchell Boyd. She smiled. When had she last really felt like smiling? Holding out her hand, she motioned to Mitch. After a startled glance at Pete, he stepped forward until he could take her hand. Still wearing an astonished expression, he let her pull him into the circle where the flashbulbs continued to explode like Fourth of July fireworks.

"Mother," Chelsea said urgently. "Listen to me, Mother. This is my friend. The one who sent me the clown and the violets. The one who kept telling me to hang in there when I didn't even believe in myself anymore!" Smiling, she leaned and pressed her mouth to Mitch's cheek. "You'll never know, Mitch, you'll never know what that meant," she whispered.

Dawn, close against Pete's side, watched this scene with an open mouth. "Pete," she cried, "what's going on? What's this between Mitch and Chelsea?"

"She's your friend, Newhouse," he said, shaking his head. "You're the one who's supposed to understand her."

Chelsea was indeed her friend, but she was also Josh's girl friend . . . or had been. Yet here was Chelsea beaming up at Mitch, her bright eyes adoring his face. Frantically Dawn looked around for Josh. He had been at her side only a moment before. "Josh," she called. "Josh!" But he was gone.

"Pete," she wailed. "Josh's heart must be broken."

He shook his head. "His isn't the first heart that Chelsea has broken," he told her. "And I'll be surprised if it's the last." His expression turned suddenly sober. "Let's get out of here. I need some of those reminders as to why I ever got mixed up in all of this."

* * *

Mom and Pop's was empty except for a solitary figure in the back booth. Pete peered back and sighed. "Necking on hold, Newhouse. Let's go."

Karen glanced up sullenly as they slid in across from her. "Make yourself comfortable," she said in a flat tone. Then, with a little face, she added, "I guess I should tell you congratulations."

Dawn nodded. "Thanks. You helped, you know."

"Sure I helped. You might even say I gave my all. I saw those shots on tv of Chelsea and Mitch billing and cooing. Let's just say it wasn't a willing gift."

"I didn't mean that," Dawn added. "What you said about my amnesia started us on the track toward the truth."

"Hypnosis," Pete explained.

Karen shrugged. "It had to happen one way or another. Like I told you, Dawn, Chelsea comes out of everything just as she goes in, pure as the driven morning snow."

Pete shook his head. "Not this time."

"What do you mean?" Karen asked, looking at him. "Smiling on tv like she was paid by the tooth."

Pete said slowly, "Deep down Chelsea will never be quite the same person again."

Karen shrugged and started to rise, but Pete laid his hand on hers. She paused, half standing, with his dark eyes intent on hers.

"Come on, kid," he coaxed. "Things will work out . . . with you and Mitch, I mean."

"Oh, Pete, I'm not sure." And she left the restaurant.

Dawn watched her go and then turned to Pete. "Do you really mean that? Do you really believe she and Mitch will get together again?"

"I don't know," Pete answered. "They've survived a lot together, though."

Like Pete and I, Dawn thought. We've survived one more thing together. We can survive anything. I have to keep telling myself that.

An exciting chapter from Chrystal Falls #6, FORBIDDEN LOVE, *follows.*

CHRYSTAL FALLS ⬧6

FORBIDDEN LOVE
Meredith Hill

The minute the coach's whistle signaled the end of the volleyball game, Dawn Newhouse started toward the locker room. Not only were her clothes dripping from the fast play of the past hour but her boyfriend, Pete Carter, was probably already waiting in the hall outside. She knew just how he would look. He would be leaning against the wall staring off into space with his face empty of expression. She loved to catch a glimpse of him like that and then see his dark, intense eyes light up and his face change when he smiled at her.

Dawn was concentrating on holding her place in line for the showers when the girl beside her went down. Dawn didn't really see her fall. She just disappeared from beside Dawn. Then someone stumbled over her and yelled angrily for her to get out of the way. Dawn, afraid she would step on her, leaned over and realized the girl on the floor was Julie Gregory and she was unconscious.

"Hey," Dawn called out. "Get back, everybody. Something's wrong."

Instead of stepping back, the other girls swarmed in closer, shutting off the flow of air and humming with questions. "Who is it? What happened? What's wrong?"

"I don't know," Dawn snapped. "But give her air." As she spoke, Dawn knelt, slid her hand in under Julie's head, and lifted it a little. "Air!" she shouted crossly.

Even as the girls stared down curiously, Julie stirred and moaned. Her eyes fluttered open and then widened as she looked up, apparently terrified by the ring of staring faces. Bracing herself on her elbows, she tried to get up.

"Wait!" Dawn urged her. "Are you all right?"

"Fine," Julie stammered. "I'm fine. I must have fallen."

"Fallen!" Perky Palmer snorted. "You fainted or something. Nobody falls straight down like that."

Dawn took Julie's hand, helping her rise to her feet. Julie swayed dizzily for a minute. "I'm fine," she said again, and tried to pull her hand from Dawn's grip.

Dawn put her arm around Julie. "Come on," she said firmly. "It's hot and steamy in there." Holding Julie firmly, she steered her away from the locker room toward the rest room, which was usually deserted just after gym.

Once inside the rest room, Julie leaned

167

against the cool tile of the wall and closed her eyes. "See?" she said. "I'm fine."

Dawn folded some paper towels and dampened them under the cold faucet. She really didn't know much about Julie Gregory. She kept to herself and didn't run with any of the crowds. She was pretty, too, in a really delicate way. Her usually fair complexion was dead white. Dawn handed her the wet towel. "Here, put this on your forehead. It might help."

Julie looked back at her with eyes as deep brown and glossy as melted chocolate. "Thanks a lot. But really, I'm fine."

"A weakling, but fine!" Karen Pickett said, coming in just as Julie pressed the cold towel to her head. "Some of us can take it and others can't."

Dawn glared at Karen. What do you do with a friend like that? She liked Karen in spite of her bluntness and strong opinions. But since losing her long time boyfriend Mitch to Chelsea Chrystal, she never had a pleasant word to say to anyone.

Karen returned Dawn's glance with an uplifted chin. "Get off it, Newhouse! Julie knows what a rotten game she played today. It was just too much for her, that's all."

"Maybe she's sick at the thought of going to the next class," Perky Palmer put in, lifting her blond hair and watching the mirror smugly as it fell smoothly down her back.

"I'm fine," Julie repeated, handing the towel back to Dawn. As she did, she turned to walk toward the door, bracing herself against the wall with her right hand. Dawn stepped ahead of her to push the door back, then caught her arm in the hall.

"Listen, Julie," she said. "This is none of my business but obviously you're not fine, and just saying it over and over won't make it so. I have my mom's car here; I'd be happy to take you home."

Julie turned, her eyes really wide and terrified again. "Oh no!" she said. "I wouldn't dare go home."

Dawn saw Pete watching from his place down the hall and signaled with her head for him to wait. Then, taking her hand from Julie's arm, Dawn challenged her, "Come on, let me see you walk."

Julie made a brave attempt, but the dizziness that had sent her to the floor made her grab at Dawn's arm. "Okay," Dawn said quietly. "If you don't want to go home, come with me anyway. We'll tell them at the office that you are going to see my mother."

"Your mother?" Julie looked confused.

"She's a doctor and they know her," Dawn explained.

"But I don't want to see a doctor." Julie shook her head. "I'm fine, I really am."

"I can see that," Dawn said, trying to coax a smile from her. "But maybe other people seeing you stagger around won't be able to."

Pete had left his spot against the wall to saunter toward them. "Something wrong, Newhouse?"

She nodded. "Julie overdid it in volleyball and fainted. I was trying to talk her into getting out of here until she feels better."

He nodded and took Julie's arm. "Come on, I'll walk you out to Newhouse's car while she checks you out at the office." Julie looked up at him, too startled even to protest.

When Dawn returned to the car and started the motor, Julie looked over at her. "Where are you taking me?"

"Not anywhere yet," Dawn told her. "But that wind is cold and wet. It's up to you. You could come to my house or I'll take you to see my mom in her office."

"I feel fine," Julie said.

Dawn stared at her steadily until Julie dropped her eyes. "Okay, I don't feel fine," she admitted. "But maybe whatever it is will go away. A flu virus, maybe. Something that's going around."

While Dawn waited for Julie to tell her where to drive to, Julie broke down as suddenly as she had slipped to the floor. With both hands in front of her face she began to cry. "But I can't tell my folks," she sobbed. "I really can't tell my folks and I haven't any money for a doctor."

Dawn reached over and touched her arm.

"The thing to do is go see my mom. Don't worry about money. And don't worry about her getting in touch with your folks. Just let's go see my mom and find out if everything is all right."

Those dark eyes were on Dawn's face again.

"There can't be anything wrong!" she cried. Dawn backed the car out and started for the exit.

"That's like saying you're fine when you can't stand up without help. The only way to be sure is to be checked."

The rain that had been threatening all day began to fall as Dawn drove across town toward the hospital. The streets were slick from an oil build-up as she drove carefully along the road beside the river. The river that divided the city breathed a wavering mist that trailed among the huge, beautiful estates on the hill across the bridge.

With Julie quietly tearful at her side, Dawn sighed. At least this looked like a problem you couldn't blame on the city of Chrystal Falls. In the months since Dawn Newhouse and her brother Josh had moved to Chrystal Falls, one crisis after another had arisen from the hatred of the Mill people for the Hill people. Dawn's friends came from both sides of the local war, Pete and Karen from the Mill, and Chelsea Chrystal from the wealthy founding family of the town. Dawn glanced at Julie, wondering where she fit in. It didn't matter. The kid needed help. Dawn pulled into a reserved staff spot in the hospital parking lot and looked over at Julie.

"Will you be all right while I go in and talk to Mom?" Dawn asked. "I'll leave the heater on."

"I might as well come with you," Julie said. Then that frightened look again. "Are you sure we are doing the right thing?"

"Nothing else makes sense."

Upon learning that her mother was busy with a patient, Dawn took Julie to the staff cafeteria for a Coke. "I don't know why you are being so good to me," Julie said, studying Dawn with those wonderful brown eyes.

Dawn shrugged. "I almost stepped on your head for starters. I am almost always nice to people after I step on their heads."

Julie giggled softly. As she did, a sudden dimple came in her left cheek. In that instant, she changed from a really pretty girl to a knock-out. Before Dawn could get used to how much a little happiness changed Julie's looks, she felt her mother's hand on her shoulder.

"What a nice surprise," Dr. Newhouse said, leaning across the table to take Julie's hand. "And who's your friend?"

"Julie Gregory," Dawn told her. "You owe the surprise to her. She passed out coming out of volleyball. I talked her into coming to see you."

"I'm glad you did." She smiled across at Julie. "Get me coffee, will you, Dawn, while I try to discover what mystery ailment our pretty friend has contracted."

Dawn was barely on her feet before Julie spoke calmly. "There isn't any mystery, Dr. Newhouse. I'm going to have a baby."